Sapphire

The Twelve Horizons of Charlie
Book Three

Melody Anne

Printed and published in the United States of America.

Published by Falling Star Publications

Editing by Karen Lawson and Janet Hitchcock

Note from Author Melody Anne

Ah, book three is complete. I struggled with book three a little bit. It was harder for me because I truly do believe in marriage. I believe it's sacred and special and beautiful. I do believe it can end, but I think when you marry someone they will always have a piece of your soul. You can hate them at the end of the relationship, but it's too late, because they've already gotten a piece of you you'll never get back.

As I dive further into this life of Charlie I fight with my own beliefs on what marriage and love and life means. It's an interesting journey. I like this journey though. I love these adventures Charlie is going on. I love the soul searching, and I love how she's finding herself.

I began this story and was working on it when I lost my mother. I had to put it down for a little while. My mother suffered from severe dementia and in the end she no longer knew who any of us were. She'd talk to me about me. But she was comfortable and she was happy, and that's the best I can ask for. She's now home in heaven and she's once again perfect. I'm grateful for all the years I've had with her. I'm grateful because it's been more than so many others get. I feel like an orphan now, but I'll forever appreciate the time I had with both of my parents. I'm a better person for having the family I have.

I'm also grateful to my friends who always lift me up, to my family who I can't live without, and to my husband who is my Bentley. We chose each other and I can't imagine living my life without him. He's patient and kind and looks at me as if I'm the love of his life. He inspires me and makes me a better writer.

To all of my fans, thank you for your support. I truly hope you're doing well. Someday, hopefully sooner rather than later, this damn pandemic will end and I can come out around the world again and see you all!!

Love, Melody

Books by Melody Anne

Romance

BILLIONAIRE BACHELORS
*The Billionaire's Dance
*The Billionaire Falls
*The Billionaire's Marriage Proposal
*Blackmailing the Billionaire
*Runaway Heiress
*The Billionaire's Final Stand
*Unexpected Treasure
*Hidden Treasure
*Holiday Treasure
*Priceless Treasure
*The Ultimate Treasure

BABY FOR THE BILLIONAIRE
*The Tycoon's Revenge
*The Tycoon's Vacation
*The Tycoon's Proposal
*The Tycoon's Secret
*The Lost Tycoon
*Rescue Me

THE ANDERSON BILLIONAIRES
*Finn – Book One
*Noah – Book Two
*Brandon – Book Three

*Hudson – Book Four
*Crew – Book Five

BECOMING ELENA
*Stolen Innocence – Book One
*Forever Lost – Book Two
*New Desires – Book Three
FINDING FOREVER SERIES
*Finding Forever

TAKEN BY THE TRILLIONAIRE
#1 Xander – Ruth Cardello
#2 Bryan – J.S. Scott
#3 Chris – Melody Anne
#4 Virgin for the Trillionaire – Ruth Cardello
#5 Virgin for the Prince – J.S. Scott
#6 Virgin to Conquer – Melody Anne

SURRENDER SERIES
*Surrender – Book One
*Submit – Book Two
*Seduced – Book Three
*Scorched – Book Four

UNDERCOVER BILLIONAIRES
*Kian – Book One
*Arden – Book Two
*Owen – Book Three
*Declan – Book Four

FORBIDDEN SERIES
*Bound – Book One
*Broken – Book Two

*Betrayed – Book Three
*Burned – Book Four

HEROES SERIES
*Safe in his arms – Novella
*Baby it's Cold Outside
*Her Unexpected Hero – Book One
*Who I am with you – Book Two – Novella
*Her Hometown Hero – Book Three
*Following Her – Book Four – Novella
*Her Forever Hero – Book Five

BILLIONAIRE AVIATORS
*Turbulent Intentions – Book One (Cooper)
*Turbulent Desires – Book Two (Maverick)
*Turbulent Waters – Book Three (Nick)
*Turbulent Intrigue – Book Four (Ace)

TORN SERIES
*Torn – Book One
*Tattered – Book Two

7 BRIDES FOR 7 BROTHERS
#1 Luke – Barbara Freethy
#2 Gabe – Ruth Cardello
#3 Hunter – Melody Anne
#4 Knox – Christie Ridgway
#5 Max – Lynn Raye Harris

ANDERSON SPECIAL OPS
*Shadows – Book One
*Rising – Book Two
*Barriers – Book Three

*Shattered – Book Four
*Reborn – Book Five

Women's Fiction

TWELVE HORIZONS OF CHARLIE
Novellas
*Diamond – Book One
*Ruby – Book Two
*Sapphire – Book Three
*Jade – Book Four
*Opal – Book Five
*Serpentine – Book Six
*Emerald – Book Seven
*Pearl – Book Eight
*Onyx – Book Nine
*Topaz – Book Ten
*Stone – Book Eleven
*Bloodstone – Book Twelve

Young Adult / Fantasy

PHOENIX SERIES
*Phoenix Falling – Book One
*Phoenix Burning – Book Two
*Phoenix Ashes – Book Three
*Phoenix Rising – Book Four

*All book links are part of the Amazon Affiliate Program

Prologue

Lights are flashing.

Words. Lots and lots of words.

What is this? I'm surrounded. I can't get away.
Where is Cash? Where is Stephy? Where is anyone?
These are all strangers.

"Why did you do it?"

"He's dead."

"You're a monster!"

I'm shoved. A stabbing pain slices into my side. I cry
out. But the noise surrounding me increases. I'm shoved
and prodded. Tears sting my eyes. I can't get away.

"Cash! Stephy!" I'm screaming, but I can't hear my
own voice through the overwhelming noise.

Someone from behind shoves me, and the front of
crowd parts. I fall on my face. Blood runs down my nose.
The wind is knocked out of me as I try to get up but
pressure is on my back. The weight grows as the crowd
hovers over me. Light is seeping away as I try to get up.
More and more weight bears down on me. More pressure,
more pain. It's too much. I'm starting to give up.

I reach out a hand and another foot slams down on it. Excruciating pain fills the side of my head as someone kicks me.

"You're getting what you deserve, you monster."

"He's dead. You killed him!"

I flutter my eyes, everything's blurry. I look up, trying one last time to rise. And then my will to fight flees. Kneeling on the ground in front of me, a satisfied smile on her lips is . . . is . . . is . . . Stephy.

"You killed him," she snarls. I've never heard such cruelty in her voice. "He's dead because of you. You lived; he died."

"No, I didn't want him to die. I need him."

"Murderer," she snaps. "You aren't even worth looking at, much less fighting for. You're going to die . . . alone, just like he did."

"I was with him. I was with him," I cry out.

"He was alone. You killed him. You killed him." She repeats this over and over before she turns from me. I reach for her. I beg her. Please. Please. Please.

She stands and walks away. The lights go out . . .

I shoot up in bed, my body covered in sweat, my cheeks soaked with tears. My body racks with sobs as I mourn the loss of Bentley once more. *Did* I kill him? Am I killing his memory? Who am I? What am I doing?

I lie down, sobbing, alone in my room. Can I keep doing this? Can I keep taking this walk into the past? Will it save me? Or will it kill me? I don't know; I don't know anything. I just know I want to run. I want to run fast and far. I need to get away.

"It's okay."

A voice is trying to break through my panic attack. I can't let go of the nightmare. I can't let go of the pain.

"Charlie, it was just a dream. You're okay."

Arms wrap around me. I'm shaking so hard I don't know how I'm being held. I should be throwing off whatever comfort is offered to me. I'm a hurricane force wind right now and I don't deserve comfort.

"Come back to me. Come back from the dark."

Slowly I return to reality. My thundering heart calms. I look up. His face is blurry. How is *he* here? How am I here *with* him?

"That's it," he says, his hand soothing the sweat from my brow. "You're okay. I'm here. I'm not going anywhere."

I sob as I fling myself at him. This is real, I tell myself. This is where I need to be. The nightmare was the fantasy. The nightmare tried to pull me under. I'm not a monster . . . or am I?

"No! Don't go back there," he says, urgency in his voice. "Hold on to me. Hold on, and let it go."

I desperately grasp at his words. I need to be okay. I grasp him as I try to let the nightmare go. I hold on tighter than I've ever held on before.

"Make me forget," I beg, tears choking me, my throat still closed.

"Yes, yes, Charlie," he says.

I fall into his arms.

Was the nightmare real or is this moment real? I don't know. I just know I need to feel . . . I need to try . . . I need to remember . . . I need to survive.

Chapter One

Who is so lucky they get to live this life I'm living? So many hate their lives, and I have to admit I've been there once or twice myself. Right now, isn't one of those times. I've never in my life thought I'd be in New Orleans during the post festivities of Mardi Gras, which go on any time Mardi Gras isn't *actually* happening, but here I am, me, Charlie Sapphire, a new name I absolutely love — thank you very much, Stephy Lawrence.

I'm shell-shocked and oddly excited. It may be the lemon drops I've been consuming since noon or it may be that I'm beginning to go with the flow of whatever comes my way. I don't care what it is. I just know that I'm having fun. A couple of years ago I had forgotten what it was like to have fun, but now I'm doing my best to figure it out.

I miss Warren. It's been four months since I've seen him, but I know it was right to leave that life behind. He was critical in helping me break free of my paralyzing sadness over losing Bentley. He was essential in my first steps out of the dungeon I'd placed myself in.

I cringe as I think about my first husband. I miss him most of all. It's odd, though, how we heal ourselves. I can't let Stephy know how right she's been all along, but time is making my heart heal. If she knows how well her planning is working then it will swell her already big head, and it might make her sign me up for an adventure I can't handle.

I'll miss Bentley forever, and now I know I'll miss Warren, though it's a different kind of absence, but most shockingly of all, through this pain, I'm finding myself. I have no clue what I'm finding, but I'm smiling again, and I'm living more instead of going through the motions like a robot on autopilot.

"This band's amazing! I'm so glad I came," Stephy shouts above the noise of the crowd and the incredible jazz music.

"I've missed you. I'm glad you came," I tell my bestie.

"Well, technically you don't start your job for another month so there's no harm in me being here," she says.

Stephy has a mission to help me find myself. She's doing this by creating entire new identities for me. This includes a new name, a new place to live, *and* a new job. I began life as Charlie Diamond, a small-town girl born and raised in Prairie Town, Oregon by a preacher father and a craft store owner mother. I married at the tender age of eighteen, and I lost my husband at the same age. I then spiraled into a sea of depression.

Stephy decided after two years she wasn't going to watch her best friend die a little more each day. That's when Charlie Ruby was created. I liked her. She was fun, she was spirited, and she began to smile more and more with each new day. She was a dancer in an incredible show in Las Vegas. She also eloped with Warren Amancio, who just so happened to own the hottest casino in Las Vegas. But, alas, Charlie Ruby had to die. She disappeared in the blink of an eye, and Charlie Diamond came back home.

The thing about changing yourself though, is that each time you do, you're not quite the same person you were before the transformation. There will always be vestiges of Charlie Ruby inside of me from here on out.

She might be gone forever, and she's truly gone as Stephy has erased her, but her memories will live on forever in Charlie Diamond.

From Charlie Diamond's cocoon, Charlie Sapphire has emerged. I like her. I think I'm going to like her a lot. It's sort of odd to think of myself as a different person, but I'm discovering if I do just that, I'm freer to act as this new person.

"Are you excited to teach?" Stephy asks me.

"I'm scared to death." I throw back the rest of my lemon drop. A new one is put before me before I can barely set my cup down. For as crowded as this bar is, the service is excellent. Of course, with the tips Stephy doles out, I understand why.

Charlie Sapphire is a gym teacher at a middle school in New Orleans, Louisiana. Who in their right mind can possibly think I should be molding the minds of the next generation? I don't know, but I have the job. I start in a month. These kids are going to eat me alive.

No!

I push this thought from my mind. Charlie Diamond might think that way, but Charlie Sapphire would never have such a thought. Stephy leans in and puts her arm around me as she holds out her phone and snaps a selfie of the two of us. She grins as she shows the image to me.

I can see the shape of my face which can't change, but I barely recognize my appearance, just as I hadn't when Stephy got her hands on me for my makeover into Charlie Ruby. I'm naturally a brunette. For my stint as Charlie Ruby, I was blonde. Now I have dark brown hair with fat mauve highlights. My hair is cut to my shoulders in a pixie like mess that looks great. I love it. It's flirty and fun, and I think it definitely makes me look twenty-five, which is the age on my new ID.

My real age is . . . I have to think for a second. I really *am* taking on my new identities. I'm twenty-one now. At least I'm of legal drinking age on both my real ID which is nowhere in sight, and my fake ID which is securely tucked away in my crossbody purse I've clutched tightly to me all night in the packed crowds.

Stephy and I are currently at the Maison Bourbon, one of Bourbon Street's oldest live jazz clubs in New Orleans. I've very clearly learned in the three weeks I've been in New Orleans that jazz is one of North America's oldest and most celebrated musical genres, tracing back to the late nineteenth and early twentieth centuries. This legendary spot is where many of the most notable jazz musicians served their apprenticeships, including Harry Connick Jr. It's only one of two jazz clubs still existing on Bourbon Street.

I get up to use the restroom and slam straight into a man. I'm pretty good at doing that. I giggle as I jump back. I look up . . . and stop in my tracks. Holy moly, this boy is fine. He's tall. I'm wearing three-inch heels, thanks to Stephy addicting me to outrageously priced shoes that are sure to kill my feet by the end of each night I wear them. Even with my heels I only come up to this man's chin.

He's nerdy too, which, shockingly, only makes him ten times sexier. He has dirty blond hair, hazel eyes, and shoulders that I want to touch. How in the world can I be ogling this man when I was just thinking about Warren?

Who am I? What's happened to Charlie Diamond? I'm not sure, but she seems long gone. After I get over my initial shock of my attraction to the man — I'm going to blame it on the vodka I've been cramming down my throat — I notice panic in his eyes.

I go from ogling him to feeling concern. "Are you okay?"

He seems to notice me for the first time, even though he's been studying me for a solid ten seconds since I tried to take both of us down in this crowded place.

"I need help," he says in a rich, smooth, aristocratic voice. My stomach stirs. The man just keeps getting more attractive. I'm disappointed he doesn't have a squeaky voice that makes me wince. I need to find a flaw so I won't think about him after I walk away — and I *will* walk away.

"Help?" I ask, confused. I know I'm a little drunk — maybe a lot drunk — and I know things are processing a lot slower, but I can't ever think of a time in my life a man's run to me looking as if I'm his saving grace.

"It's my brother's bachelor party and I'm trying to stay calm, keep it together, and not run out of here screaming, but this is my idea of pure hell," he says as he throws a hand in the air, his other hand staying on my shoulder. He isn't exactly grabbing me, but more like holding on to me like I'm a raft and he's about to go under. Unlike Rose, I feel I can't let go for him to sink to the bottom of the sea.

"I'm confused."

He sighs. "I'm not a social person. I love my brother with all of my heart, and I want this to be a great night for him, but if he or his friends make one more comment about me being single, or calling me gay because I'm not married with ten kids, I might have to punch my brother and all of our friends in the face."

I'm trying to keep up, I'm *really* trying, but he's not making a ton of sense.

"You're gay?"

He throws up both hands this time. "No," he tells me, "there's nothing wrong with it, to each their own, but no, I'm not gay. I just don't need a woman to *make* me a man." He finishes with this sexy growl that makes some butterflies jump in my stomach.

"I agree. Some people like to be alone. I like my own company more than being with other people most of the time."

He looks at me like I'm the savior of the world at this comment. He grabs my shoulders again and squeezes as he gives me the brightest smile I've ever seen. I'm a bit blinded. I wobble just the slightest, assuring myself it's the vodka, not the man's hands on me, not the smile, and certainly not the sexy Clark Kent glasses.

"Will you please laugh as you look at me like I'm the most interesting man on the planet and then write down a number on this napkin?" He pulls out a napkin and pen from his pocket. The nerd factor just grew a bit, and I find him even sexier. "Write a fake number. I told those guys I could get any woman's number I wanted and then I stormed off. I wasn't thinking." He hangs his head for a second before looking at me with a little bit of shame and a lot of determination. "I caved to the mob."

His last words make me laugh . . . hard. "I like you, Clark."

"Clark?" he asks, clearly confused.

"Yep, you look just like Clark Kent before he rips open his shirt." I eyeball his button-down shirt, wondering if it would be as easy to rip open as it seems in the movies. I find I want to try it. He might be the one looking crazy, but I'm the one feeling the emotion.

He looks at me as if I might actually be insane for the briefest moment, and then he throws back his head and laughs. When we meet each other's eyes again, we're both smiling. That clench in my stomach grows tighter. His hands are still on me. I like them right where they are.

"I've never been compared to Superman," he tells me. "I like it."

"I've never been asked to give a fake number," I respond. "I like it too." I take the pen and napkin from him and write my *real* number down. I don't know why. I'm sure he's going to toss it, and I'm sure we're both going to forget all about this exchange when we wake up with hangovers in the morning, but for now, I'm liking this exchange quite a lot.

I don't know what comes over me, but I hand him the napkin and then I take his cheeks in my hand. I look over to the table of howling men and smile. Then I get up on my toes as I pull Clark Kent to me. The shock on his face is priceless.

"Let's give them a show." I'm expecting to give him a quick kiss. We *are* in New Orleans after all. People are kissing all over the place. When in Rome . . .

I touch my lips to his . . . his shock evaporates as his arm wraps around me and he pulls me in tight. The short kiss I'd planned doesn't happen. His mouth molds over mine and I forget all about the game we're supposed to be playing as his tongue traces my bottom lip. I gasp as I open to him, my stomach tight, my core tingling, and my nipples aching as they're crushed against his solid chest.

His tongue slips inside my mouth and we start a tango unlike any dance I've ever experienced before. I'm on fire, inside and out, my skin is tingling, my ears are buzzing as the sound of sweet jazz washes over us. I tune out the whoops and hollers, and my only focus is on this stranger, this man I'm calling Clark Kent. I don't care. I want more.

His hand slides down my back and he presses into me, showing me there's more hardness to his body than just his chest. I can feel his arousal pressing against my core. He tugs on me, and my leg comes up as I try to get closer to him. I've just been wondering who I am, and in the space of seconds I've forgotten what country I'm in . . . and I don't care.

When his mouth breaks away from mine, I pull back slightly, gasping for breath. Where in the hell had that come from? Had Clark turned into Superman? His glasses are a bit askew, and his hazel eyes are smoky. He looks as if he wants a lot more — I know the feeling.

"Well, well, well, where in the heck did you come from?"

The laughing voice of Stephy wisps past the fog in my brain. I don't turn away from Superman — he's no longer Clark Kent, he's officially transformed — as I try to get my bearings. I'm glad he still has his arms wrapped around me, because I'm afraid my legs just might fail me.

"I don't want to interrupt, but you might want to find somewhere more private to carry on since it looks as if the two of you are about to get naked."

This time Stephy's words penetrate my lust-filled haze. It seems to have done the trick for my mystery man too. He loosens his grasp on me.

"I didn't know you had it in you," a male voice says. Superman is knocked into me as the man in question slaps his back. Superman turns and glares at the intruder.

The kiss sobered me. I'm still feeling damn great, but I realize where I am and what this entire scene is about. I paste a siren's smile on my lips as I turn to the drunk man next to Superman.

"Nice to meet you. Time for me to run though." I lift a painted red nail and trace it down Superman's chest. "Call me." His mouth drops open the tiniest bit. That kiss had to have rocked his world at least half as much as it rocked mine. I blame the jazz. The damn sexy music has most definitely caused more than one baby to come into this world.

I take Stephy's arm and we walk away. She's looking at me with respect and humor. It feels good to be Charlie Sapphire. I'm already loving this new role I'm playing.

"What in the heck was that? It was hot as hell, that's for sure," she says. I move past the bathroom. I need air. I need to get out on the street. I don't say anything. For one, it's almost impossible to hear as we move past the band, for another, I'm still trying to catch my breath.

We make it to the street and I inhale deeply. There's music out on the street that's nearly as loud as in the bar. People are walking arm in arm as beads are thrown. It's always Mardi Gras in New Orleans. There are masked folks and happy couples. There are those in barely any clothes and some covered from the tips of their heads to the soles of their feet. I see skull painted faces and brightly painted bodies. I see it all — and now, I'm a part of it.

"Talk now," Stephy says.

"He was on a mission to get a phone number so his bachelor party group would leave him alone. I don't know how the impulsive kiss turned into a tornado of lust," I admit.

She throws her head back and laughs. She then stops and turns me so we're face to face. She looks so dang happy. I'm not sure what in the heck I'm feeling.

"That was amazing. Charlie Sapphire is a siren," she exclaims. I might've been embarrassed but the people walking past yell out their approval of her words then keep on moving down the crowded street. "New Orleans will be the best adventure yet."

I find myself smiling. "I agree. I like letting go. I like not being Charlie Diamond." It's true. Charlie Diamond's life is too restrictive. Charlie Sapphire's life is a movie. I want to be in the movie . . . and this is my set.

"Okay, new rules," Stephy says as she moves me over to a new bar and smashes her way to the front where we're immediately served. We pause our conversation as we take our drinks back out on the street and keep moving.

"What rules?"

"You are one hundred percent Charlie Sapphire now. You have no past, only a present and a future. Don't let Charlie Diamond seep in like an angel on your shoulder. I want to have an adventure, and I want to go to another wedding."

I gasp at her. "I'm already married." That realization is a splash of cold water in my face. I'm suddenly mortified that I've kissed another man when I still have a husband. I might've left him, but that doesn't mean we're divorced. Marriage is sacred — even a Vegas marriage. What have I done?

"Well," she says dramatically as she waves her hand in the air. Someone from a balcony up high tells her to take off her shirt. She looks up, winks, then keeps walking. There's no way she'll do that. We do have some of our faculties still in place even in this party atmosphere.

"You aren't married," she finally tells me.

"What do you mean?" I'm not sure how I feel about this. I feel *very* married to Warren Amancio. It was a good marriage even if it was never meant to last. I don't regret a minute of it.

"It was never legal. The paperwork was all wrong," she says with a wink.

"Does Warren know?" How would she know this? How do I not know it?

"What matters," she tells me, ignoring my question, "is that you're free to live as Charlie Sapphire with no worries, no guilt, and no rules. You *will* live each and every single day to the fullest and continue to be this vixen I'm getting a glimpse of."

My mind's spinning. What does all of this mean? Am I *really* free? I smile. I *feel* free. I've done nothing wrong. Just because I've kissed Superman doesn't mean I don't value my past. Just because I've found desire in my body doesn't make the past desire any less real, or any less impactful on who I've been or who I am now.

"You're right," I say. "I'm free."

I down the rest of my drink, throw my hands in the air, and shout, which causes several people to cheer with me. It's great to be a part of the crowd.

Just then a throng of people split as a marching band moves down the street, trumpets blowing, drums beating, and beads flying. And like a hero coming from the fog, Superman immerges in the middle of a group of men. Our eyes connect and I'm singed. Stephy laughs beside me.

"Let's join the wedding party," she says with laughter. I don't know what's about to happen, but I'm not about to turn and run. Superman's eyes are latched onto mine. The air is burning all around us, as if I'm in a movie and I'm about to have that climax moment. That makes me smile bigger. I wouldn't mind a great climax. I'm Charlie Sapphire, siren of the seas and man killer.

I smile, and let Stephy leads me toward the group of men. The night's about to get interesting, that's for dang sure . . . and I'm not going to fight it one little bit.

Chapter Two

There's a full-on symphony creating its newest masterpiece inside my head. I've heard of people saying this before, but I've never experienced it. That is until I came to New Orleans and drank half the liquor in town. I keep my eyes shut as I try to put the pieces together from the night before.

I remember Stephy and me at the bar. My body tenses as I remember Clark Kent. Nope. Hold that . . . Superman. He transformed right before my eyes, shirt undone, and red cape flying in a glorious manner. I remember leaving. I remember Stephy declaring I have to embrace my new life. I remember Superman reappearing from the fog like the savior of us all.

My body stiffens as a sigh escapes — from the person next to me. Flashes from the night before flit through my mind. Laughter, parties, dares . . . a wedding.

No!

No! Are you kidding me? No. It can't have happened. I finally open my eyes and stare in shock. The glasses are gone, the face is utterly relaxed, and the chest, oh, holy hell, the chest is on full display as the sheet rests just below the very sexy happy trail. There's a bump that tells me the slightest provocation will wake this man up. It's Superman . . . and I'm in his bed . . . and I don't even know his real name. Carrie Underwood's song about just that flashes through my brain before I shut it down. I don't need vocals right now with the drums already pounding, even vocals as good as hers.

I shift as I lift my arm, and then squint when a ray of sun hits the bling on my finger. I look down and see the diamond encrusted band resting there. I check both hands. Holy hell, it's on the left side. More flashes explode in my brain. It can't be.

No.

It doesn't matter how many times I shout this word in my pained brain, I know what happened. I can't be so lucky as to black it all out like so many others seem to do. Right as I have this thought, I push it away. It wasn't all bad. Okay, none of it *was* bad. It was crazy, it was foolish, it was certainly impulsive, but it *wasn't* bad.

I start moving. Superman groans as I slide out from beneath his arm and scoot myself from the bed. I'm completely naked, and as I get to my feet, I realize I'm sore . . . in all of the good places. I move on tiptoe to the bathroom of the large hotel suite. Clothes are scattered all over the floor. I gather them up, hoping I've found everything. I close the door to the bathroom then turn on the light.

I look as terrible as I feel. I can only glance at myself for a second in the mirror. My makeup is smeared beneath my eyes. My hair looks as if I've been sexed all night, and I'm not going to double check, but it appears there are a few hickeys on my neck and chest. Who in the hell am I? I've never done something this rash before. I'm going to murder Stephy for playing along. Sure, I'm an adult and I could've stopped it, but she's my best friend and is supposed to be the voice of reason, not the person egging me on.

I quickly scrub my face, then take a one-minute shower. I can't find a brush, so I finger-comb my hair, then throw on my clothes, noting that my panties are long gone. They were a bare wisp of fabric anyway. I'm sure they're shredded. I'm going to have to do the walk of shame in a short dress with no underwear. I've utterly demoralized myself and I deserve the walk everyone is aware of.

I open the bathroom door, grateful there's no squeak. I find Superman still soundly asleep. There are miracles in the world; I've just witnessed one. I tiptoe back into the room and grab my shoes, not at all excited about putting the heels back on my sore feet, but I have no choice. I'll do it when I'm down the hallway out of Superman's hearing range. But doesn't Superman hear through walls?

I have to cover my mouth quickly as I stifle a giggle. What's wrong with me? I'm in this situation, I feel like crap, and my brain's still making jokes. I really am morphing into Charlie Sapphire. Or maybe I should call myself Lois Lane.

I'm about to leave when I wonder if I should leave the man a note. No. It's better to simply disappear. Then I see his pants. I move over to them and reach into the pocket. Sure enough, there's the napkin with my phone number on it. I hesitate. Then I sadly shake my head and grab it, throwing it into my purse. It's better to pretend this never happened. I look at Superman one last time, regret filling me . . . then turn and walk from the room. I have a best friend to find.

It's only seven in the morning and there aren't many people out. I manage to find a cab after about ten minutes of walking on my screaming feet. I'm grateful that Stephy and I decided to stay in my condo instead of on Bourbon Street. I hope she'll be back at home. I have plenty of time to think about stuff as the ride takes twenty minutes, even without a lot of morning traffic.

When I arrive home, my head's still pounding, but I'm getting used to it. I come inside my condo and head straight to the kitchen where I take Advil and drink about a gallon of water. I decide I'm going to lie on the couch and let the pills kick in before I wake up Stephy, who is snoring in the guest room. I guess she made it home just fine. I doubt there's some stranger she's calling Superman lying in *her* bed . . . but then again, you never know.

The pills take the sharp pain off of my headache, and I can't wait any longer. I march into Stephy's room and plop down on the bed next to her. She grunts as my leg hits hers.

"Ugh, I need coffee," she says with a groan, not bothering to open her eyes.

"There's a pot brewing."

She suddenly seems to come wide awake as she sits up and looks at me from head to toe. I'm lying next to her with my arm over my face. I'm wearing the dress from the night before, but I kicked off my shoes as soon as I walked in the front door.

"Soooooooo," she says, drawing out the word for what feels like an hour. "Where's the new husband?"

There'd been a part of me hoping I'd been dreaming as I remembered the night before. Her words confirm that I've forgotten nothing. I slowly sit up while glaring at Stephy.

"How in the world did we do what we did?"

She laughs. The wench *actually* laughs.

"Well, there were a lot of bars, a licensed official, and a lot of hands greased, and poof, a Parish marriage license was produced."

"Wait! What?" I gasp as I look at her.

"It was a beautiful wedding right in Cemetery Number One. Not only did you get married in the oldest, most famous, most haunted cemetery in New Orleans, maybe even the world, but you did it right at the grave of the Voodoo Queen Marie Laveau. I thought it was a bit morbid at first, but then I realized how dang cool it was. A lot of hands had to be paid to make that happen. The historic, sacred place is protected."

"Forget about the place. Did I marry Superman? Like, *really* marry him? How? You can't just marry someone on the spur of the moment unless you're in Nevada," I point out.

"You can do anything you want if you have enough money," she says with a wave of her hand. "I need Advil and coffee." Before I can stop her, she jumps up and leaves the room. She's moving awfully good for someone who'd been up partying all night. I'm not as quick as I follow her. She has both of our cups of coffee ready when I finally arrive.

"How did we go from partying in New Orleans to me getting married in a cemetery?"

"The guys were goading Superman, which is what stuck for him after you called him that, and saying he's never done an impulsive thing in his life. He told them they were full of it. I think one said to prove it, then dared him to elope in a cemetery. You said, deal, then laughed as you leaned against him and batted your eyes like a teenage girl. Then the two of you laughed for nearly a minute. After that all it took were some phone calls . . . and voila, we had a cemetery wedding."

"That's all it took?"

"Yep, it was great. I might have to have a cemetery wedding myself. I loved every second of it." She sighs as if it's the most romantic thing in the world. I realize I've now had three weddings. One more and a funeral and I'm a movie. Hadn't I been thinking the night before that I wanted to be in a movie? I think so, but it hadn't been *that* particular one.

"How do we get it annulled? I can't exactly be married to a man whose real name I don't even know." I drink my coffee. My head's clearing and I'm already feeling better. Maybe it was the incredible night of sex. Sex does a body good. Though, it's odd; I'm almost happy about the impromptu wedding before I spent the night with a man I don't know. It helps me feel less like a tramp. I don't know why I have the thoughts I have. I guess my father's lessons really stuck about marriage and sex. I again wonder what's wrong with me and why my mind goes where it goes.

"Let's allow it to all sink in," she says. "I have to get back home tomorrow and I want to play tourist for one more day." She's already moving around. Both of our headaches must be clearing. "I need to go to Café du Monde. A person hasn't really visited New Orleans until they go there and have a café au lait and a beignet."

When Stephy gets into this mood there's no getting her out of it. We'll talk more on fixing yet another marriage. I won't see Superman ever again. I feel a pang at the thought. I liked him. He made me smile a heck of a lot. But, he doesn't fit into my new life. I don't even know who he is. It's time to be Charlie Sapphire and that means . . . okay, I don't know exactly what it means, but it means something.

"Okay, we'll fix it later."

"Deal," she says.

A new day begins.

Chapter Three

"What in the world should we call you? Ms. Diamond? Should it be Diamond? Ruby? Sapphire? Fraud?"

"Objection!" Cash shouts as he stands, hands on his hips, eyes blazing as he glares at Mr. Hart. It's more for show than actual outrage. He knows this man's words can't hurt me. He also knows he needs to respond so the jury can see how out of line the man is.

"Agreed. Watch it, Mr. Hart," the judge warns.

I look at the judge who seems to constantly be fighting a smile. It's unlike anything I've seen before with a judge. They are always so stoic. I like Judge Croesus. He's someone I'd normally want to befriend.

"I'm simply confused, Your Honor. Ms. Diamond talks about how much she loves her first husband, but she seems to forget him, and *all* of the other men she leaves in her ashes as she moves on to a new identity and a new life. She talks about finding happiness. Is it okay to find your own happiness at the expense of others?"

Cash starts to object again, but I hold up my hand. "I'd like to answer this." All eyes are glued to me. It's something I'm starting to get used to. It's quite a difference from the wallflower I'd once been.

"Go ahead," Mr. Hart says as if he's doing me a magnanimous favor. I smile at him. He's not a bad man, he's simply trying to do his job, and it has to be *very* difficult in my case. None of this is anywhere near black and white. Along that vein, though, life is *never* black and white. It's messy and colorful and subject to change.

"I think we all focus too much on the negatives in this world. We can either be sad that we fish for twelve hours and only manage to catch two fish, or we can be elated that we have the opportunity to supply our own food and have something, rather than nothing, in our hands at the end of the day," I say.

Mr. Hart throws up his hands and turns to the jury rolling his eyes. He faces me again. "Do you want to explain that to those of us who don't speak in metaphors?" he demands.

"I lived extremely negatively for a very long time. I played the victim. Why had my life turned out the way it had? Why was I being punished? Why was a great man ripped from this world when I was allowed to stay? It was *all* about me. And then I woke up." I can't tell them Stephy woke me up. I'm not going to say anything that will get her involved in this mess.

"*How* did you wake up? How does that have anything to do with your crimes?" Mr. Hart presses.

"I realized my life is very much a blessing. Each day I take in breaths, each day I climb out of bed and can walk, and each day I smile is a blessing. No, my happiness shouldn't be earned on the backs of other people's pain, but I *can* find happiness in others. We can share with each other, and we can grow together. We can learn to live, and we can even attempt to fly. There's nothing wrong with that. I have loved, and I have lost. I have lived and I've come close to dying. You might not like my story, but it's *my* story. I don't care if you like it. I'm telling it for me . . . *not* for you."

"You're telling it in the hopes of not spending the rest of your life in prison," Mr. Hart corrects.

I smile at him. "If I go to prison that will just be another new identity. It's okay to remake ourselves.

There's nothing illegal about that. People change their names all of the time," I tell him.

"There's a legal process to do that," Mr. Hart tells me.

"Have you ever stolen a piece of candy, Mr. Hart?" He looks at me as if I'm insane. I continue. "Remember, we're in a court of law where lying can land you in jail. Have you ever in your life stolen a piece of candy?"

Mr. Hart's brain is spinning. I can see it in his eyes, calculating, trying to figure out where this is going. I can also see the jury leaning in just a bit closer. Mr. Hart also sees this. He reads a room well. He realizes if he doesn't play along, he's going to come across as a villain. He doesn't want to play my game, but he's being forced into it.

"Yes, I've stolen a piece of candy, but not since I was six years old," he tells me. "By that age, I clearly knew the difference between right and wrong. Have you learned that difference?" he shoots back at me.

I tilt my head and think about his question. Have I learned that lesson? "I think right and wrong can be subjective," I tell him. "If I go into the store and steal a piece of candy, I'm one hundred percent in the wrong.

However, if a mother runs out of food, and has no money, but has hungry children, are you going to punish her for stealing food for her babies?"

"Yes," he says. There's a gasp in the courtroom. I don't know when I became the lawyer and he the witness, but I'm enjoying the process. Maybe law school is in my future. I also notice Judge Croesus isn't saying a word. He looks more as if he wants to grab some popcorn and cotton candy and enjoy the show.

"Really?" I don't know how to follow up with this. It wasn't what I'd been expecting him to say. Who in their right mind condemns hungry children?

"The mother could've asked for help, she didn't need to take something that wasn't hers," he calmly tells me. Before I can respond he continues. "The world turns to hell the moment we start erasing the line between right and wrong. Do we excuse someone stealing food, but not stealing diamonds? Couldn't the same logic be used? A diamond ring will buy a lot more loaves of bread so if her children are hungry shouldn't she take something bigger to get more food? Most people would say no. If you make it very clear that wrong is wrong, then there are no gray areas."

I nod at him. "I like that thinking." He and the jury seem shocked by my acceptance. "But even in a world of black and white there have to be exceptions. Otherwise, we're all animals without hearts. The animal kingdom will do what it takes to survive. They will steal, they will murder, they will chew off their own paw if trapped. We've become a civilized people who have compassion and heart. Sure, there are those in this world who abuse that belief in humanity, but I think there are far more people like me who see color in every picture."

"You make a good speech, Ms. Diamond, but the bottom line is you've used men to get what you want. You've broken the law, and you must pay for that. If everyone gets to live lawless, there won't be order in this world," he tells me.

"Who decides the laws?" I could ask what laws I've broken but I don't need to go there. Cash is sitting back in his chair, looking relaxed. He has no problem with me duking it out with the prosecutor. He trusts me. It's one of the things I love most about him.

"We the people decide the laws," Mr. Hart haughtily says.

"I don't think so. I think that might've been the way in the beginning, but I think power changes people. There's a ton of corruption in this world, and because of that no one wants to obey *anything* anymore. There used to be a very simple understanding of right and wrong. I don't think that line in the sand is so clear anymore. It breaks my heart."

"You've broken the law so I can see why you'd say that," he tells me.

"I've broken what *you* deem as the law. I disagree with you." I pause for a long moment, then smile at the man who's trying to send me to jail. "I guess at the end of this trial we'll see whose law is right and whose is wrong."

"There is no wrong or right," Mr. Hart says as he tries to not get flustered. I'm undermining him and he doesn't like it one little bit. "The law is clear. Bigamy is against the law."

"And you've defined bigamy?"

"No, the *law* defines bigamy," he tells me, coming back to his confident, arrogant self.

"You haven't proven bigamy."

He gapes at me. I keep my satisfied smile in place. "That's because you're very sneaky, and you're taking a hell of a long time telling your story. I'm a patient man, though, Ms. Diamond. The jury is patient as well. You can play your games all you want. In the end you *will* be found guilty." His confidence has most likely shaken many opponents. It's not working on me.

"Patience is a virtue," I tell him. "My father preached that lesson for my entire life." I look out and smile at my father. "I was very lucky to grow up in such a loving home. Both of my parents taught me a lot." I turn back to Mr. Hart.

"You might not like my story, and you might not agree with my choices. You, however, will *not* degrade the time I've spent with the people I've loved. Each person in my life has been essential to who I am. Just because I've deviated from the norm of society doesn't make me a monster, and it doesn't give you the right to judge me. I've lived my life to the fullest. I'm going to continue to do so, no matter what you think about it."

I lean back. I've said what I want to say. If the jury doesn't like it, that's too bad for them. If the reporters don't like it, I don't care. The only opinions that truly matter to me are those of the people I love the most. I need them in my life. The rest of the world can fade away and I'll be just fine. For that matter, I'll be okay even when this life of mine ends. Because then I'll go home to where I'm meant to be.

"Since this is never going to end until you finish your story, why don't you continue," Mr. Hart says. "You're on to the next man quite quickly. Number one has died, number two wasn't legal. You've married number three in a cemetery. I'm curious how you're going to get out of this one." His words are snide and vindictive. I decide I wouldn't mind being an attorney, but not a DA. They are too dang mean. It doesn't matter, though. This man can't hurt me. He can, however, make himself look like more of an ass than make me look like a slut. I got married. It was legal. It was right.

"I thought you'd never ask." I love thinking about Superman. "I didn't see Superman for a month after we were married. What a big surprise it was for me . . . and for him when we met again . . . and in a shocking place."

There's a chuckle in the courtroom that doesn't please Mr. Hart. He also doesn't like the name of Superman. But at this point in my story I didn't know my husband's real name. I might just think of him as Superman for the rest of my life. He did rescue me after all . . . and he most certainly did make me fly.

"Please tell us how you and *Superman* came together again after a month," Mr. Hart says, his voice dripping with judgement.

"Glad to . . ." I climb back into the past . . . sometimes it's my happy place, and sometimes it causes utter despair. In the beginning there's a lot more happy. In the end I'm beginning to accept closure. Here we go again . . .

Chapter Four

"Welcome back to school!"

A loud cheer erupts from the hundreds of kids sitting in the school auditorium as the new principal of the school stands in the middle of the gym and throws his hands in the air.

I'm scared. These kids can eat me alive.

I'm also excited. I like the principal. He's young, eager, and ready to try new things. Too many kids don't enjoy school, and this man wants to change that attitude. He wants them to learn and have fun at the same time.

"We have new staff this year. Are you excited to meet them?" he asks the kids. There's another cheer. It's amazing how excited you can get people by simply being positive and acting as if even the worst things in life are positives. It's all about attitude.

"Me too. I hope they didn't all apply from the local sanitorium. But just in case, you might want to turn in your homework on time. I don't know what will happen if you don't," he says as he looks around in mock fear, making the kids laugh.

I didn't come from a local insane asylum, but I'm not really who I say I am either. I wonder if that counts. How many people are being deceptive about who they really are? Then again, what is deception? Don't we get to choose who we want to be? To a point, I decide. I can't be a mermaid, but I can put on a tail and swim to my heart's desire if I want to act like one.

"Let's bring all of our first-year teachers on up," he says. I inwardly groan.

He begins calling names. Mine's the fourth one. I stand, looking down at my feet as I move up beside him. I take in a breath, paste a big smile on my face, and look at the crowd. The kids are going wild. I know many people before me have compared schools to zoos, but since this is my first time in this setting since I left middle school, I haven't realized how accurate they are.

These kids look as if they are all hyenas about to pounce. I can do this. I can make it through. The principal calls out a few more names, some of the teachers shifting uncomfortably, and some dancing and jumping around.

It's a good mix of introverts and extroverts. I think I sit in the middle of the road.

"Now I have a surprise for all of the teachers and for you kids," Principal Long says. I take another nervous breath. I'm not a fan of surprises.

"We're going to skip the lessons today. You've had all summer to run wild and we have to ease into school. With that being said, we're going to have our new gym teacher, Ms. Sapphire, lead us all in a game of dodgeball, kids versus teachers' edition."

The kids leap to their feet, screaming in excitement. I meet a few of the gazes of some of the eighth graders and realize I'm about to be pummeled. It isn't often kids get to throw balls as hard as they can at their teachers and not get into trouble. I might be a little bruised by the end of the day. I quickly recover from my shock and decide to go with the flow. I walk up to Mr. Long and take the mic.

"Do you think you can beat us?" I ask, looking far more confident than I feel.

"We'll demolish you," a kid shouts. I look at him, and decide he's in the wrong school. He looks big enough to be a starter for the NFL. The gleam in his eyes says this is the best day of his life.

"You can try, but we old people have a few tricks up our sleeves," I say. I'm actually getting more into it as I speak. The saying about faking it 'til you make it is actually pretty accurate. "Everyone to their sides."

I hand the mic back to the principal as a thundering herd of bison comes rushing off of the bleachers. The teachers head to one side of the gym, the kids to the other. The balls are brought out, and there's a standoff. I try to move back farther, but feel myself getting pushed forward.

There's a flash of red, and I barely have time to turn before I see the ball coming straight for my face. Thank goodness I've played on a ranch my whole life. Instinct kicks in, and I catch the ball right before it shatters my nose. I hold on tight, then turn and find the same huge kid grinning wickedly at me. I wink, and that wipes the smile off his face. I quickly undercut the ball, and slam him in the hip so quick he doesn't have a shot. He gives me a look mixed between adoration and shock.

I feel good.

I haven't always been the most coordinated of people, but I've always enjoyed exercise and hard work. I might just make it out of this without any broken bones. My confidence is knocked out from beneath me when a ball slams into my stomach taking my breath away. Evil laughter follows me as I move to the back of the gym with all of the other teachers who've been knocked out before me. At least I wasn't the first to go. Mr. Long is still in, pummeling kids left and right as both sides cheer on their teams.

I sit down against the cushioned back wall, and the air shifts. I've felt this before. It's such an odd sensation. I see a pair of legs in front of me, and then I look up, shock and . . . excitement running through me.

It's Superman.

How? Am I imagining him?

"Well, well, well," a voice taunts. I look over to my left, and see Jesse, one of the men from the bachelor party gang. What is going on?

"Did the two of you have that whole night planned?" Jesse asks, a huge grin on his face. I must look in shock. "By your expression on your washed out face I don't think either of you had a clue the other worked here. This school year just got a hell of a lot more exciting."

"What are you doing here?" Superman asks. "At least I know your name now." He slides down so he's sitting on one side of me with Jesse on the other. No one is paying the least little bit of attention to us. Laughter, grunts, groans, and screaming is echoing through the gym.

"I'm teaching," I say lamely. He looks as if he's not quite sure of what to say. Then he grins, that sexy grin that goes straight to my gut. He holds out his hand and waits. I automatically take it.

"Sterling Worth, middle school science teacher," he tells me. "It's great to officially meet my wife. Do you happen to know where our papers are? I tried to find you, but got nowhere. The phone number, real or fake, was gone when I searched for it."

I gape at him. I haven't even thought about the papers, or the phone number I took back. I told Stephy we had to take care of the marriage, but then I got busy. Was I reluctant to file for an annulment? That couldn't be. I don't even know Superman . . . Sterling, I correct myself.

"Charlie," I say. I don't add my last name. He knows it now since Mr. Long announced it to the entire gym. I find I don't want to lie to this man. I'm not lying, I tell myself. I *am* Charlie Sapphire, middle school teacher. I've taken on this role, and I want to fully submerge myself in this act I'm really enjoying . . . at least until the curtain call comes.

"I was disappointed when you were gone in the morning. I had a great night," he says.

I realize I can freak out, or I can go with the flow. Hadn't I decided just a short time ago to go with the flow? Do I want to be the old Charlie or the new? Definitely the latter.

"I had a great night too. I don't often get married at midnight in a cemetery without being struck by lightning."

He throws his head back and laughs. "I don't often get married within a few hours of meeting someone. But . . . it was a bachelor party."

"I thought you were an introvert. You aren't acting very upset about this situation," I tell him. I'm still looking for flaws in him, but I still can't find any. I like Superman . . . a lot.

"I've had a month to think about things. I can be upset, or I can loosen up as my brother often tells me. There are many marriages that are arranged all around the world. We can just pretend we're royal. When do you want to start trying for the first royal birth?"

He says this with a straight face, and for just a moment I panic. I in no way want to have kids. I'm not mother material. Some women are born to be mothers, and some can't even find themselves, let alone raise a new generation. I fall into the second category.

"I like the practicing, but I'm in no way ready for the responsibility," I say.

"Hot damn, you two were made for each other. I'd totally think this is all a set-up for your brother, but there's no way you've been secretly dating this woman without any of us finding out. I think you've met your match," Jesse says.

"Maybe," Sterling says. "I'm not displeased right now."

"I don't think I am either."

"Let's get that changed to you're *definitely* not displeased," Sterling says. I want to lean into him and see if his lips taste as good as I remember them tasting. I want to see if the sparks igniting inside of me will burn just as hot as they had on our one and only night together. The screaming kids all around us remind me I can't do that . . . at least not yet.

"Would you like to go out on a date with me, Mrs. Worth?" It's so strange to hear him call me by his last name. Had I put that on the marriage license? I've never seen it. I realize with bright clarity it's in the hands of my evil best friend. What has she done with the papers? Did she file them? Is this man truly my husband? I don't know.

I check out Sterling, not just ogle him. He really is handsome. His Clark Kent glasses give him an air of nerdy sophistication that makes me all warm and gooey. His broad shoulders, flat stomach, and strong legs make me want to run my hands all over him. His eyes, oh, his hazel eyes burn into me. I've been in love, and I've been in lust. What I feel for Superman confuses me. I don't know how to respond to it, or how to react to it. I like this man. I like him a lot. But why do I? Is it just lust? I guess I'll find out.

"It depends," I say after a long silence. He raises a brow as a wisp of hair falls over his forehead. I automatically reach up and brush it back. Electricity shoots through my fingers. Yummy.

"What does it depend on?" he asks. He looks just as turned on as I feel.

"What the date is. I don't like boring adventures."

"Oh yeah, this girl's a keeper," Jesse says. I've forgotten he's sitting with us. I smile at him before turning back to Sterling.

"I guess I'll have to come up with something great then. How about Friday after school?" he asks.

It's Wednesday, so that gives me nearly two full days to calm my nerves. What will he have us do? I don't care. I decide to jump on in. "It's a date."

He beams at me.

Before we can talk more, Mr. Long calls out, giving the kids a victory over the dodgeball game. They scream like a pack of monkeys as they take a victory lap around the gym, taunting all of the teachers. Superman climbs to his feet, then holds out his hand.

I take it and he easily pulls me to my feet. I stumble into his chest, then look up as my breath is stolen from me. I find myself wanting to close the short space between us. I need to taste his lips again. I have no doubt it will happen. Will I have to wait until Friday? What's happened to my self-control?

Before I do something foolish, a group of kids rush around us, breaking us apart. We're separated as the assembly continues. I guess I'll have to get through the next few days and see what chapter comes next in my story. I'm beginning to learn I don't have power over my life. I think someone else is writing my story. I hope it's a great author.

Chapter Five

What does a person do when they are panicked? That's easy, call your best friend.

As soon as I get home from school, I call her and demand she get her butt to New Orleans. I have questions for my best friend, and I want to ask them in person. She quickly agrees. I then pace as I wait and wait and wait . . . which actually doesn't take long for her to arrive.

"I need out of this house," I tell her.

"I'm game," she says. I barely get the housekeys in my pocket before we rush to the Uber and make our way downtown. Luckily, we find some open seats.

We're on a swamp and Bayou tour. She only gets to be here for a day and informs me that each time she comes she wants to do something new and exciting. Being pretty dang good at planning dates, even friendship dates, I pick something outside where we can enjoy the scenery and still visit.

"You've been here for three hours and have refused to talk shop." We're sitting in the back of the boat as the sun sits low in the sky. I've had a full day of teaching, though the first day doesn't really count as it was almost entirely a game day. But still, I understand my free time is going to be limited with a full-time day job. I need to get right to business.

"Ugh, you can be no fun at all sometimes," Stephy tells me with a laugh. "I'm looking for alligators."

"What have you done with my marriage license? Is my marriage real?"

Stephy turns and grins at me. "Oh, it's *very* real," she says. "Why do you ask?" This is when I notice the gleam in her eyes. I gape at her.

"You *knew* he worked at the school," I accuse. "How could you hold that information from me? How in the world did you know? Did you know him ahead of time? Was it all planned? Did you pick that school on purpose?"

Stephy throws her head back and laughs with glee.

"Of course I knew he works at the school. He's been there for seven years. As a matter of fact, he's been in

New Orleans for most of his life. He left just long enough to go to Ohio State University with a full-ride scholarship playing for the Buckeyes," Stephy says. I'm shocked at this.

"He played football?" I should have a lot more to ask than that since it seems my bestie knows far more about my husband than I do. There's a shocker . . . not. I *did* marry the man after knowing him for only a few hours.

"He was good, *really* good. I looked up some old videos. He was a defensive end. With those shoulders I can see why."

I agree with her assessment. The man has incredible shoulders. For that matter, his entire body is delicious. "He's a science teacher, though. I like how nerdy he is, but I don't picture him as an athlete too." I normally love football players, so I don't understand why I'm disappointed that he played college ball.

"He can be a nerd *and* an athlete," Stephy points out. "Those are the sexiest men of all, you know. They can rule the world and defend your honor at the same time."

"When did you find all of this out?"

"I knew who he was before you said I do, but I researched him a lot more after I came home. I can't have a psycho married to my bestie. I *do* have standards," Stephy says.

We're traveling deeper into the secluded bayous across the Mississippi River. The guide is speaking about Cajun culture and the myth-laden swamps, but I'm not paying much attention. I'm going to have to take the tour again. It really is great history, and I love knowing how this amazing place I've been born and raised in came to be what it is. Right now, though, I'm more interested in learning about the man I'm currently married to.

"Stephy . . ." I begin, but she gasps as she pulls out her phone to snaps a picture. The boat stops and there's a group of alligators right beside us. I'm not an alligator fan — not at all. While she leans over, I find myself jumping up onto my seat and scooting to the middle of the boat. I'm not taking any chances. "Get back here," I hiss, trying not to draw attention from the alligator. It might come up and eat us. She keeps snapping pictures.

"Didn't you see that video of a kid's birthday party when someone was feeding an alligator and it grabbed her hand and dragged her into the pool? Some guy had to save her."

"That rarely happens. Most of them are just big old puppy dogs," Stephy says. I shake my head vehemently.

"He looks nothing like a dog. He looks hungry." A shudder passes through me. "Why in the world do I put myself into these situations with you? I don't like being scared."

"You do it because you love me and you know it's a fun adventure. We aren't going to sit in our safe little houses and not live our lives," she tells me, just as she has a million times before. I love sitting in my house. I have to admit, though, I'm becoming more addicted to adventure the more I get out and see the world.

I realize Stephy is listening to the guide, so I patiently wait as the cityscape transitions into wetlands that seem to go on forever. The guide is pointing out alligators, egrets, raccoons, snakes, and the most giant nutria I've ever seen. We have the overgrown rodents in Oregon too, but not this big. They look as scary as the dang alligators — well, almost as scary. With all of the creepy stuff, though, the incredible Louisiana terrain is lush with greenery and abundant with wildlife, some friendlier than others.

"The Cajun people have populated this region for over two hundred and fifty years," the guide tells us. He shares stories of popular Cajun music, bayou lifestyles, and culinary traditions. "Did you know the Cajun people created Louisiana's signature gumbo? What was a necessity with limited food has turned into an incredible dish loved all around the world."

"It's true, I love a great bowl of gumbo," Stephy says.

"You love anything with meat in it."

"Yeah, I could never be a vegan. I have mad respect for those who follow their principles, but these teeth were made for sinking into nice juicy meat," she finishes as she points to her canines.

I laugh, just as I always do with my bestie, once again realizing I'm never going to stay irritated with her for more than a minute or two. I love her too dang much. That's how it goes when you have the world's greatest best friend.

We pass by the Barataria Preserve showing some remarkable wetlands and how the area is preserving tens of thousands of acres of nature. There are bayous, swamps, forests, and marshes all being preserved. We then pass Jean Lafitte National Park. The ride is over before I'm ready for it to end. But finally I'm able to get Stephy's full attention.

We take a cab to Antoine's Restaurant on St. Louis Street in the French Quarter. It dates all the way back to 1840 and is the oldest restaurant in New Orleans, and not only that, but the oldest to be continuously operated by the same family. That's not just for New Orleans, but it's the longest one-family-owned restaurant in the entire country.

"I'm starving," Stephy says.

"Well, if I feed you and get you drunk, maybe you will settle down long enough to speak to me." I wink and laugh.

"I think there's a great possibility of that happening."

The waiter comes and we place our orders, deciding to go with their four-course dinner. When dining at the oldest restaurant in town, you can trust the specials. The place knows what it's doing.

Our Domaine Gautheron Chablis wine comes out along with escargot au gratin. I wrinkle my nose as I look down at the snails on my plate.

"I don't know if I can eat this."

"Don't be a wuss. You've eaten cow balls before," she says, diving right into her dish.

I force a gag back. "Yeah, but those were fried. This is a snail on my plate." I'm poking it.

"It's sauteed in brandy with spinach and leeks. You'll be fine." She takes a bite and sighs.

I glare. "I'll eat whatever is placed before me *if* you start talking." It's a challenge.

She throws back her head and laughs. "Okay, deal. Bottoms up."

She finishes her wine and holds up a hand for a refill. This dinner is certainly going to cost us. Stephy doesn't worry about money, but I do, even though I have a ridiculous amount of it in my checking account. Bentley's been gone for three years and I still don't feel as if the money is mine. I'm not sure I ever will.

I take a bite of the snails and surprisingly, I actually like them. I'm not going to admit it to Stephy though.

She's right way too much of the time. I wrinkle my nose as if this is really tough for me. I finish the food, then drink my wine.

"Do you have my marriage papers?" I ask. We have a few minutes before our next course comes out.

"I didn't bring them. They won't do you any good anyway." I start to protest but she holds up a hand. "Why don't you see how it goes with Sterling? If it doesn't work out, we'll take care of the marriage. I like Superman though. I think he's an incredible man, and I think you should have fun with him. It might be true love."

I cringe at those words. I can't imagine having another true love. We only get one in a lifetime, I've decided.

"I know that look. Wipe the thought straight from your head. I know Bentley is the love of your life, but he's already home. You have to live your life while you're still visiting this earth. When you get to heaven you can do what you want then."

"I'll want to be with Bentley when I get home." I don't want to feel sad, but the weight of his loss pulls me down again. I hate this feeling. "So, what's the point of dating anyone else if it's only for a little while?" It's a question I ask myself quite often.

"The point is that you have a lot of years left on this planet and you can still love Bentley and love someone else too. You can't be alone forever. We aren't meant to be on our own. We need to have a partner," she tells me for the thousandth time.

"I have you," I remind her.

"That's not the same as a husband, a lover, a twenty-four-seven person that's with you through the good and the bad."

I laugh. "That pretty much describes you . . . minus the lover part, of course."

It's her turn to laugh. "I'm a damn fine lover, but that's off the table with us."

"Duh," I say. "But seriously, why do we feel we need a partner so bad? I love being lazy at home in my pajamas. With a partner I have to compromise and dress up. I'd rather just be alone."

She looks at me for a while. "When you're with your true equal you can be yourself."

"I had that with Bentley. I don't think I'll have it again."

"You will. I know you're the marrying kind. There's no other option for you," she says.

"*You're* still alone," I point out.

"I'm not you, but when the time is right I'll find my perfect match," she assures me.

We're interrupted as our waiter comes with our second dish — alligator bisque — with a new glass of wine, this time a Willamette Valley Pinot Noir. It's sort of nice to have wine from home. I love Willamette Valley Wine. It's the one my mom always has in the house for the rare occasions she has a glass.

I dive into my soup. It's delicious. "I like eating alligator a heck of a lot more than I like seeing them alive with their beady little eyes glaring at me as they plan to eat me alive," I tell Stephy when the waiter leaves. She leans back and laughs, spitting a bit of her wine out.

"Don't make me choke," she gasps. "They don't eat you alive. They drag you under water first and get you nice and tenderized." I feel my stomach drop. What a horrible death.

Stephy suddenly grows serious, going back to our conversation. "Back to our conversation. I'm not always alone. I just haven't found a man I want to be with forever. If I'm with a guy and it's not working, I end it."

"You aren't allowing me to do the same."

She raises her brows. "Really?" she asks. "I keep telling you to give these men a *chance*. When you *are* for sure done, I support you. All I say is to at least try, to spend time with them, to open yourself up to the possibility of love. Are you attracted to Superman?"

"Yes." There's no way I can lie about that.

"Do you find him funny?" I nod. "Sexy?" I nod again. "Then give the man a chance. He's already your husband. What do you have to lose?"

"I'm giving him a chance. I'm going on our first date together." The words sound so funny. We both start giggling. I'm going on the first date with my husband. I definitely have to write this down in my journal. My life truly is a movie . . . or a book. It can't possibly be real.

Giving up on getting the paperwork from Stephy, I decide I'm going to give Superman a chance — a real chance. I don't think he can possibly win my heart, but why not enjoy the journey of a good flight together? It can't hurt me. I do like him. Maybe that will change — maybe it won't.

Stephy and I finish our dinner of lamb striploin and an amazing dessert of blueberry cheesecake, then take a very tipsy ride back to my place. Thank goodness for cabs. I might regret all of the wine when I have to be in a hot gym all day with yelling kids. But time out with my bestie is worth the pain of a headache the next day.

I'm finally excited for my date with Sterling. Let's see if he comes out as Clark Kent or as Superman. Either way I'm most certainly a winner.

Chapter Six

STEPHY

"Your Honor, we'd like to call Stephanie Lawrence to the stand."

Well, it's about time. I have a lot I'd like to say, but the bottom line is that I'll stand by Charlie's side through thick and thin, through good and bad, and through hell or heaven. She's my sister, my best friend, and my other half. She's Charlie and the world would suck without her.

I smile as I rise from my bench in the audience. I see Charlie's head whip around and panic rise in her eyes. I wink at her and am so proud when she pushes the fear back, not willing to show the jury there's anything to be worried about with my testimony. She hasn't given anything away. She's managed to tell her story without telling how she's gotten her ID, or how everything has disappeared when one life ends and a new one begins.

It wouldn't matter if she does slip up, though. I can't be caught. I'm sure that's how many people bending the law feel, but in my case, I have zero worries. Heck, I have less than zero worries. My head is held high as I move to the witness stand. I have nothing to fear. I'm good at what I do. I'm a genius when it comes to the computer. I'm not bragging, it's simply a fact that I've been blessed with a gift. I'm grateful every single day for the freedom my love of computers has given me.

I sit then raise my right hand as I'm sworn to tell the truth, the whole truth, and nothing but the truth. I inwardly smile. Isn't truth subjective? Some say a lie is a lie is a lie. I say the truth is the truth is the truth. We live in our own truths of what we deem right and wrong. I believe in God, I believe in humanity. I believe those in power aren't the almighty last defense. They don't get to decide my fate. That's between me and my higher power.

Besides, when Anne Frank was hidden in the secret annex of a home for seven-hundred-and-sixty-one days, the people hiding her were *technically* the criminals, and the soldiers looking for her with the intent of killing her were the law-abiding ones.

Is there anyone in their right mind who'd now say that the law as written would've been a good idea in Anne Frank's case? If they do, they are wrong on so many levels it would take a whole new book to describe it. Sometimes, the right thing to do is fight the law, sometimes fighting back is our moral imperative. Sometimes civil disobedience keeps the politicians running our lives walking the line they should be walking. They aren't our rulers, they are our representatives.

I like thinking of it this way. That makes me a warrior, a crusader — Wonder Woman. I've always believed I should've been born an Amazon woman. Maybe I was and I was stolen at birth. Now, if I can only get my flying abilities zoned in, I'd be perfect.

"Can you state your name for the transcript?" Mr. Hart asks.

"Stephanie Ava Lawrence."

"And how do you know the defendant?"

"She's been my best friend since before we were in school."

"So, you're an expert when it comes to Ms. Diamond?" he questions.

"I'd say I know her better than any other person on this planet." I pause and look out at Charlie's mother and father. "She has incredible parents, but we all keep secrets from our mom and dad." The room chuckles at my statement which is very true. Mrs. Diamond nods at me. She really is a second mother to me. I might not have survived the loss of my own parents if it hadn't been for Charlie's to fill in for Bentley and me.

"What's your occupation, Ms. Lawrence?" Mr. Hart asks. He doesn't want the jury or audience to fall in love with me. It's too late. I've made it my mission in life to have everyone like me. I've realized over time that it's a simple formula to get people to like you — you respect others as much as you respect yourself, and they're sure to respect you. They might not always love you, but they'll like you as they won't be able to find fault in your actions.

"I've worked for Google remotely for the past thirteen years," I say.

"How old are you, Ms. Lawrence?"

I laugh. "Isn't it rude to ask a lady that question?" I fire back. There's another chuckle in the audience, this one louder. The judge hits his gavel a couple of times.

"Order," he warns. The laughter gets stifled.

"Please answer, Ms. Lawrence. This is a court of law, not a comedy club," Mr. Hart admonishes.

I lean my head to the side and raise a brow. "It sure seems like a circus to me, and one not very carefully planned," I fire back.

"Your Honor, I might need to treat this person as a hostile witness," Mr. Hart snaps.

"Oh, I'm a lover not a fighter. There's no need for hostility," I tell him with a wink.

"Ms. Lawrence, Mr. Hart is correct. This isn't a circus. Let's keep the acts at a minimum," the judge says.

"I like you," I tell the judge. I barely keep myself from winking at him too. He's cute, has a total Sean Connery look going for him. I want to ask him to say, *Welcome to the Rock* in that sexy as hell voice only one actor has down to a science. I have a feeling he might go for it after a few drinks.

Judge Croesus just looks at me with a deadpan expression. It doesn't make him any less hotter. I might have a thing for older guys with white beards. Maybe it's a celebrity crush thing, or maybe I just like mature men.

"How old are you, Ms. Lawrence?" Mr. Hart asks again between clenched teeth. I turn back and look at him as if I've forgotten he's there. I actually almost did. But I need to get on with things.

"I'm thirty," I say.

"So, you've worked for Google since you were seventeen?" he asks in clear disbelief. He obviously hasn't carefully checked into my background. That's his mistake for making assumptions. "How did that occur?"

"Well, I broke into their system when I was fifteen and told them what they were doing wrong. Someone liked me there, and for the next two years we chatted. I was offered full-time remote employment at the beginning of my senior year in high school. I gladly accepted."

"You broke into their system?" I can see the wheels turning in his eyes. He's trying to put the puzzle pieces together. Luckily for me I can be cocky, because all of these suits find it far too unbelievable that a young lady such as myself could be capable of forging documents from the government, and most certainly think I'm unable to break into highly secure government agencies. Their ignorance works for me.

"Yes, I'm not sure how that happened, but I'm good with numbers." I twist my blonde hair in my fingers, making myself look about as dumb as a typical freshman going to a party school like Syracuse University. I barely contain myself from adding some valley-girl talk. I don't want to push my luck. If I act too dumb, they'll realize it's just that, an act. It's a fine line I'm used to walking.

"What do you do for Google?" he asks.

"Are you sure you want to know all about my life. I promise you it's not that exciting, and the story might take quite some time." I pause for a moment as I look at Charlie. "And since my bestie over there has found her voice and really likes to chat it up, you can imagine where she learned it from. I could be up here for weeks." Outright laughter follows these words. I can see Judge Croesus pushing down his own smile as he bangs his gavel again. He clears his throat.

"As council has pointed out, this isn't a comedy club, Ms. Lawrence, please answer the questions without the extras," he tells me.

"Sure thing, Your Honor," I say. I give him my full smile, which I've been told can light up a football stadium. Women who don't use what God's given them are fools. I'm where I am in life because I'm smart. I get what I want without hurting anyone, but by using all that's been given to me — my brains, beauty, brawn and sassiness.

I sit and wait, and Mr. Hart seems irritated. "Please answer," he tells me.

"What was the question again?" I ask. I know exactly what the question was, I just like infuriating this pompous man.

"What kind of work do you do for Google?" Mr. Hart repeats, his composure regained. He takes a little walk in front of the jury, his hand in his pocket, a smile on his face. He seems as if he's an indulgent parent. It works for him.

"I analyze data that comes in. Some might find that very boring, but I find it fascinating. Did you know that the average person worldwide spends six hours and fifty-nine minutes a day consuming content including phone, TV, and other forms of digital media? The average time online alone has risen to one hundred forty-five minutes per day. That's a lot of opportunity for targeted ads. We spend far more time on social media, mostly using phones that are clutched to us like lifelines. I bet everyone in this room has itchy fingers wanting to grab their cell phones as I speak just because I said the word. If we forget our electronic crutches when we leave the house, a lot of us have panic attacks."

I'm about to continue when he holds up his hand. I've bored him, just as I've intended. The jury isn't bored. They look slightly horrified. Most people are when they realize the amount of time they waste online. It's scary. Our phones track our time on the devices and how much time we spend on each app. I'm not proud of some of my bad habits on the phone, but then again, I work hard, so what I do in my free time is my own business. That's scary too. It always makes me want to go out for a run.

"You seem to have been every place Ms. Diamond shows up, no matter what her name is," he says. I don't say anything. He hasn't asked a question. He quickly realizes I'm not going to be easy to manipulate. "Why is that, Ms. Lawrence?" he adds after a long pause.

"Have you ever had a best friend?"

"How is that relevant?" he fires back.

"It's very relevant. If you've never had a best friend, this questioning is going to go on and on and on and on as a big waste of time for me and for everyone else in this room, and without any understanding from you at all." This makes his eyes narrow.

"I'd very much like for you to answer the questions I present. You *are* under oath and required to answer," he tells me.

I give him my most taunting smile. "I'm up here because I *choose* to be." My smile switches back to the innocent one meant to appeal to the jury. I'm infuriating Mr. Hart. Charlie has to cover her mouth to stop her laugh from coming out. She knows me quite well, and she knows when I'm having fun pushing buttons.

"Did you help Ms. Diamond as she broke the law?" Mr. Hart snaps.

"No," I say simply and honestly. I don't believe we've broken the law. See? The truth is the truth is the truth.

"You've done nothing with all of your computer skills to help the defendant illegally change her name, give herself fake degrees, and marry multiple men with the records mysteriously disappearing?" he fires.

"Fake degrees? Illegal ID? Disappearing records?" I'm wide-eyed innocence. I'm good at playing the victim when it's necessary. I'm also good at not perjuring myself. "I haven't seen you show any of this so I don't know what you're speaking of." The flare of anger in his eyes makes my smile grow a bit brighter.

The court won't find any of those papers because I'm damn good at what I do. They won't find a thing they can use against Charlie. They've only found what I've allowed them to find. And though I'm being questioned, I can see in Mr. Hart's eyes he finds it very unbelievable I'm capable of something this big. Good for me and good for him. He's a fool. Even if he somehow figures it out, he can't prove it. It must be very frustrating to deal with someone like me on the stand. I almost have sympathy for him . . . almost, but not quite.

"We *will* find something that sticks, Ms. Lawrence. If you know of anything it's far better for you to speak up now before getting buried alive in a falling building," he tells me.

I widen my eyes and gasp as if I'm shocked. "Don't you think that's a very tactless statement considering the disasters happening around the world right now? There have *literally* been people buried alive in the past weeks due to collapsing buildings from storms, earthquakes, and avoidable disasters." I donate every time there's a natural disaster as I want to help where I can. I know this wasn't what he meant, but the more I can throw him off, and the more I can make him appear the monster, the better it is for my best friend.

"I . . . that . . ." He stops. He knows he's in a bad position.

"Just tell me why you've gone to each location Ms. Diamond's been traced to," he says in frustration. I haven't been a cooperating witness at all. And as for him treating me as hostile, he sucks at it.

"That goes back to the best friend comment. If you'd ever truly had one, you'd realize that a best friend is your other half. A best friend is the one person in the world who knows you more than any other. They don't judge you when you're wrong. They stand by your side through thick and thin. They cheer you on when others tell you it's impossible, and they comfort you when you fail, encouraging you to try again. You might fall in love, you might have a family you will love, you might even have siblings. But you *choose* your best friend and nothing short of a solar flare wiping out the planet will break up the bond of that relationship. If she's somewhere I *will* go to her. It's that simple."

"Even if she's breaking the law?" Mr. Hart pushes, obviously happy to get one question answered. I'm only answering what I want and how I want. It shouldn't take him long to figure that out.

"She hasn't broken the law," I say. Then I paste that innocent smile back on my lips. "But if she did break the law, even if she committed murder . . ." I pause for a long moment as the jury members sit up to hear what I have to say. "I'd come and help her bury the body. That's what best friends do for each other."

There's a gasp from some reporter in the audience. I can see the headline now: *The uber wealthy Stephanie Lawrence has committed to helping bury the body with her best friend, the runaway bride, Charlie Diamond.* At least no one can say our lives are uninteresting.

"So, you're telling this courtroom right here and now that you'd cover up any of Charlie Diamond's crimes?" Mr. Hart asks, looking like a cheetah pouncing.

"Of course I would . . ." I sigh as if I'm very disappointed. "*If* I could, of course. But in this world of technology, isn't it impossible to get away with anything anymore? They used to say if there were no witnesses there was no crime. But in this day and age, there's a witness everywhere you turn. You can't walk down a simple street without a dozen cameras on you. They're in the stoplights, on the storefronts, in each person's pocket, on people's heads as they drive, ride bikes, skateboards, and walk. Our lives are in living motion. We now live in a world that's one long movie. We've officially become the Truman Show. Isn't it fun?"

"People do get away with crime," Mr. Hart points out.

I cock my head. "How would you know?"

He looks confused. "I'm not understanding where you're going with that," he admits.

"Did a crime happen if no one saw it, or are you just speculating?"

He looks as if he wants to wring my neck. I used to get that same frustrated look from my twin many times. I've always been crafty. It's another of my gifts.

"Crimes do happen without witnesses, that doesn't make the guilty any less guilty," he snaps.

"I thought the law is that we are *all* innocent until proven guilty." I'm not helping his temper.

"Of course we are," he snaps.

"Well then"— my sweet smile in place — "*prove* a crime." It's a clear challenge and everyone in the courtroom knows it. Mr. Hart isn't pleased. It doesn't take him long to regain his composure though.

"I intend to, Ms. Lawrence. I certainly intend to," he says.

"Good luck." My voice is low and sweet. This time the laughter is muzzled from the crowd. The red towel has been tossed to the ground and I don't think the man's smart enough or strong enough to pick it up.

"I'm done with Ms. Lawrence for now. She's obviously here to play games instead of taking this matter seriously," Mr. Hart says. He sits down and immediately looks at his notes as if he doesn't have a care in the world. But I know he's seething.

Cash stands up and I feel a flutter in my stomach. Hot damn, this man is fine. The first time I laid eyes on him I was horrified at the clench in my stomach. He is, after-all, one of my bestie's husbands. That's completely taboo in our book. It should be in everyone's. It's way gross to double dip. And I consider it just that when a man is shared, no matter how much time has passed since they were together.

However, once Charlie confirmed nothing sexual happened between her and Cash, it opened a whole realm of opportunities. So far, there's been a lot of flirting, and a heck of a lot of desire, on my part for sure, but nothing beyond that. Will I allow something more to happen? I'm not sure.

I'm no angel. I like flirting. I *like* men. I'm not a virgin, but pretty damn close. I haven't led half the life Charlie has led. Some parts of me are envious, but not in a jealous way. I love her, and I love that her wings have spread. What holds me back is the thought of giving my life over to one person scares the living crud out of me. I've seen beautiful relationships, and I've seen horror stories. Maybe I need to quit watching the show *Snapped*, it might be skewing my view of relationships a little bit.

"Ms. Lawrence, thank you for being here," Cash says. Oh, the rich timbre of his voice is enough to make all of the women in the room sigh. What was wrong with my bestie that she didn't fall head over heels in love with this man? I'm afraid to ask her, but I'm certainly grateful she didn't.

"The pleasure is all mine," I say, and Cash chuckles.

"How would you describe Charlie's character?" he asks. Our eyes connect and I feel as if it's just the two of us in the room. I can picture us throwing all of the papers aside on his table and seeing what all the fuss is about with table sex. I clench my legs together as that tingling turns to a burning feeling. Is Cash a good lover? I want to find out.

"She's the best person I've ever known. She's kind, loyal, works hard, loves her family, and my brother knew she was the one from the moment they first met. He loved her from day one, and his last words were to tell her just that." I choke up at the end of my words. I don't like thinking about the day Bentley died. It was heart wrenching. It changed both Charlie and me forever.

"I've heard many people say the same. Can you answer why she moved around the world?" he asks. There's zero resentment in his tone. He had his time with Charlie, and I can't wait to hear their story. She's tight-lipped for now at least. I might have to wait along with everyone else to find out what happened between the two of them, shocking since she tells me everything on a day-by-day basis.

"She was utterly broken when Bentley died. I watched as she withered away more and more each day for two solid years. She knew she needed to make a change, or she was going to die and break her promise to my brother. She decided to live. It's no one's business how she decided to do that."

"I agree with you. Who gets to decide what's right and wrong? Should all women just sit back and wait to be told what to do? If a man did what Charlie did over the past decade he'd be hailed a hero. A movie would be made about him, other men would buy him drinks at the bars, and we wouldn't be sitting in court. Is this sexism at its finest?" Cash asks.

I can't help it, I laugh. "I think this is a joke. It's nothing more. I'm okay with it, though, because I love this woman and the world now gets to know her almost as much as I do. What a gift that is." I mean it. Charlie's worth knowing. Her life's been an adventure, and I love watching her soar.

"Has she broken the law?" he asks.

"No," I say with confidence. "She's as clean as a newborn baby after her first bath."

Cash laughs. I smile. I can picture having a baby with this man. That thought washes all color of my face. What in the hell had I just thought about? I don't think of babies, and I certainly don't yearn for them. Maybe I'm getting sucked into this too much. I should run — I won't. I shake off the absurd fear.

Cash finishes up, and I stand. I give the judge a sexy smile, then swing my hips as I walk away. I know who I am; I've known for a very long time. That doesn't mean I don't get lost once in a while. That doesn't mean I don't feel real emotions. It just means that I climb back on my feet and try again. I'll do it each and every day. I stop at Charlie's table.

"I love you."

"You better," she says, something she's said our entire lives. I squeeze her fingers, then walk to the circus seat section of the courtroom. Let the show continue. It's only going to keep getting better.

Chapter Seven

Why am I nervous? Maybe because even though I've now been married three times I've never really dated. That seems odd. I remember being so judgmental of those who had multiple marriages. Why are we, though? There are serial daters, those who choose to never get married. What's the difference? I guess because marriage is sacred, at least it is to a lot of people.

I'm pacing, waiting for Sterling to pick me up. No idea where we're going, but I hope it's fun. I'm discovering I like to have fun. I had a lot of great times in Las Vegas. Even though I loved it there, I grew restless much sooner than I thought I would. I had to leave when I knew it was the right time. I've promised myself to have no regrets, and hopefully I can keep that promise. But I need to be careful which promises I make — even to myself.

Sterling pulls up in front of my condo, and I take some deep breaths. I don't want him to know I've been pacing in front of the door waiting for him. He's ten minutes early. I'm glad because I can't stand that fashionably late thing so many people feel they need to do when going out on a date.

He rings the bell. I take a breath, and another, then open the door. He takes my breath away as he does each time I see him. He's dressed in a pair of dark jeans with a button-down blue shirt, the top two buttons undone. His hair is a bit messy as if he's been running his fingers through it, and there's a five o'clock shadow on his chin and cheeks. He looks absolutely edible.

"You're beautiful," he says as he hands me a rose bouquet. I smile. It feels good to be told I look good.

"Thank you. I was thinking you're dang sexy. Come in so I can put these in water."

He follows me inside and I wonder if we should leave the house at all. We're already married, and I haven't been alone with him in over a month. My body knows what it wants even if my mind's fighting these desires.

"I like this place," he says.

I look at him, and his words contradict his look. "No, you don't," I say with a chuckle. He laughs with me as I pull a vase from beneath the sink. Stephy sent me a welcome home bouquet when I arrived so, thankfully, I have one.

"No, I don't," he admits with a sheepish grin. "I'm not a city boy."

"But you live in the city." I finish messing with the flowers and turn to face him as I lean against the counter.

"Not really. I work in the city and I do things, but I live on the outskirts with my neighbors farther apart. I like lots of land surrounding my home where I can be loud if I want, run around naked, or not worry about what my neighbors think. I also like to be able to look at the stars. You can't do that in a city. The lights drown out the gorgeous night sky."

"I agree with you on that. Stephy, my best friend, and I, have spent many, *many* nights lying in the grass for hours, looking at the sky and planning adventures as we count the stars. I miss doing that."

"Where did you grow up?" I hesitate. I don't want to lie to this man. Would Charlie Sapphire's answer be different from Charlie Diamond's? Oregon is a big place. Would I be giving too much away if I tell him?

"I grew up in a small town. I'll keep the mystery alive for now of where that is." I give him a flirty wink, wondering if he's going to be upset. He looks at me for a bit, then shrugs.

"I guess our entire relationship has been mysterious," he tells me. "Though, I was born here, and haven't been away much at all, just long enough to go to college. This is home and this is where I'll always be."

"Do you have any desire to travel?" I'm a little disappointed. I think of Oregon as home for sure, but I've loved my traveling adventures, and they've only just begun. I want to leave the country, but it also scares me to do just that. There's comfort in staying where you know the culture. Maybe I need to rip off the bandages and see the whole world. Maybe it will make me a better human being.

"I take some trips in the summer, but I love home the best," he says.

I wonder if we have that much in common. The person he's saying he is aligns perfectly with Charlie Diamond. But does he align with Charlie Sapphire or any other Charlie I've been or might be?

"I want to see the world." I pause. "I don't know though. I'm still finding myself." That's a hundred percent the truth. "What are the plans tonight?"

He grins as if he means it now. "You'll have to trust me to find out," he says. He holds out his hand. I don't even hesitate as I take it.

The evening is warm but I bring a sweater just in case, however I don't need it as we step from my condo. He helps me into his truck, and then we start driving to downtown New Orleans. I haven't been there in a while.

I look at my condo and decide he's right, I don't like the place much. It's sufficient. It's very nice, actually, in a great area with a pool and all of the amenities, and lots of shopping within walking distance, but there's no separation from the neighbors. Maybe I still am a small-town girl at heart.

We chat as we head downtown. He parks his truck and we walk hand in hand until we stop at a statue. I look at him and raise my brows.

"We're going on a tour," he tells me.

"What kind of tour?"

"A haunted tour," he says. I shudder.

"I'm not a huge fan of being scared."

"I figure if you get scared you'll be left with no choice other than to hold on to me," he tells me with a wink.

"Mmm, that might not be so bad." He wraps an arm around me and it feels good. It feels better than good.

"I might be a little scared and have to hold on to you," he tells me, making me laugh.

"I somehow doubt that's true."

More people gather around us and then our guide shows up in a long, spooky coat and a fancy top hat. Everyone always seems to be in character here in New Orleans. I like it.

"Hello ladies and gentlemen," our guide says. "I'm Emanual and will be your guide this evening. Exploring New Orleans can be an intimidating quest on your own, but lucky for you, you have the best guide to take you on this journey filled with ghosts, voodoo, and vampire hunts. We're going to see some of the city's most eerie sites as I tell you tales of adventure many haven't lived long enough to tell."

There are several nervous chuckles from the crowd as the guide looks behind him as if he's telling secrets that might get him into trouble. I love it. I love the authenticity and the magic of the evening. This is going to be great.

"Are you scared yet?" Sterling whispers in my ear.

"Very. You should probably hold me tighter." His arm pulls me in closer. I don't mind being frightened anymore at all if this is at the end of the rainbow.

"We're going to be walking so I hope you've worn comfortable shoes tonight. We'll see the LaLaurie Mansion and New Orleans Pharmacy Museum, which has a dark past and articles of old. You must stay close though, because people have been known to disappear in this city filled with voodoo magic, ghosts, and vampires. It's a full moon tonight, so make sure to listen for things that go bump in the night."

A couple of giggles sound out in our group, and I snuggle even closer to Sterling. I know I'm safe. I'm not superstitious, but there is an eeriness in the way our guide's speaking and the darkness surrounding us.

We begin walking as Emanual regales us with stories. Our first stop is at the New Orleans Pharmacy Museum.

"Louis Dufilho, America's first licensed pharmacist, opened what is known today as the first Pharmacy Museum, all the way back in 1816. Now, this former apothecary shop hosts an assortment of medical exhibits from the past. Beware though, in the city of legends and magic beyond our comprehension, that you might go inside alone but have a ghost at your side on the way back out. Enter at your own risk."

"This man is good," I whisper to Sterling. He chuckles.

"Yeah, I don't spook easily and I find myself hesitating to step inside," he admits. This makes me laugh a little hysterically. This is all a show. I need to remember that.

We step inside where several other tourists are looking around. It's really quite beautiful even if it's scary. We wander the first floor seeing the cases filled with opium bottles, perfumes, cosmetics, and voodoo potions.

"The reason this is the first apothecary shop in the entire United States is because it was established by our very first licensed pharmacist in the US as I said outside. It's also said to be haunted due to the atrocities that took place in this very building," Emanual explains. Some of our group have split off but I really want to hear the history. I'm fascinated by all history, the good, the bad, and even the ugly. It's remarkable how far humanity has come in only a few hundred years.

"What questionable medical practices?" I ask. Emanual looks at me and I realize his eyes are so dark they're almost black. It sends a shudder down my spine. I think he's wearing contacts, but man is his costume right on. He deserves a heck of a big tip.

We move over and look at a display of surgical instruments, medicines, and old prescription bottles.

"Louis J. Dufilho, Jr. was the first to pass the licensing examination and became America's first licensed pharmacist. During that time a pharmacist was more like a doctor today, diagnosing and treating health conditions. Many medicines were made by blending plants, herbs, minerals, animal parts, and insects as ingredients. These were crushed together to make pills, edible wafers, liquids, salves, and injectable medicines. Back then they also utilized leeches, opium, and of course, voodoo remedies."

"That sounds a bit scary knowing what we know now about medicine, but it doesn't sound questionable with the knowledge they had." I walk closer to the display.

He smiles. "Just wait," he tells me with a wink. We move outside into the stunning historic courtyard where many weddings and events happen. We look around a bit before we head upstairs. It's even spookier than downstairs.

"This is where the living quarters, physician's study, and . . . sick room were," Emanual says.

"If we're going to get ghosts clinging to us then this is where it's going to happen," I tell Sterling.

"Do you think we need the Supernatural tattoos?" he asks me. I whip my head around in shock.

"You watch that?" I gasp.

"Doesn't everyone?" he replies.

"You have to admit there are some things in that show that seemed like nothing more than a story, but now seem a bit more real."

"I don't know if I'd go that far, but there are some things that make me think," he says. Then he leans in closer. "Like I'm wondering if some of our government officials are those leviathan things that have been duplicated and are coming to eat us all up."

I can't help it; I laugh hard at this. My fear is dwindling. Emanual starts speaking again and I quiet my laughter and listen. I love this history more and more the longer we're on our tour.

"When the property was sold to Dr. Dupas, the pharmacy began losing its popularity as gossip began making the rounds that he was engaged in unethical and experimental pharmacology. He was mixing tonics that didn't seem to work and using addictive components such as cocaine and heroin in his prescriptions. It's also said that he added voodoo rites and rituals to his practice."

"I've heard many were doing the same in those days and that most people didn't have a problem with it." I know some fun history.

"You're correct. People liked their drugs, even back then, probably more back then because life wasn't easy," Emanual says. "But, what hurt him was rumors spread that he was performing medical experiments utilizing razor-sharp drills, scissors, and scalpels that were unnecessary. They say he allegedly experimented on pregnant slaves, utilizing unknown drugs that had their origins in voodoo or used poisons that resulted in birth defects, miscarriages, and even deaths of mothers and their babies."

"That's horrible," I gasp. "Why wasn't he stopped?"

"Ah, that's the big question. Rumors also said neighbors saw patients enter this very building . . . but they never exited. When too many filed reports, the doctor was questioned. He suggested they'd simply moved away, probably to France."

"That was it? They just took his word?" I've seen evil in this world, but this seems unbelievable to me, even for the 1800s.

"For over a decade, Dr. Dupas continued with his ghastly experiments until he finally died in 1868 from complications of syphilis," Emanual finishes.

"Good. That's at least a tiny slice of karma coming back his way." I'm outraged over his crimes. How disgusting. How many people throughout time have gotten away with such awfulness? Was he the first known serial killer?

"Was syphilis his punishment, or was it the disease that had driven him mad?" Emanual asks.

"I don't care. I only care that he paid. He's hopefully still paying in hell."

"I agree," Sterling says as he holds my hand.

"It wasn't until after his death that his crimes were fully realized. They discovered far too many remains of his missing patients buried in this very courtyard behind the building."

A shudder passes through me as I realize I was just standing out there when a hundred and fifty years ago people were buried in the same place. I want to bring flowers, do something to honor their lives. I feel tears welling.

"Everyone agrees that Dr. James Dupas was evil . . . they also agree he's the most common ghost within these walls. They say his soul is so evil he can't ever leave. The image of a short, stocky, middle-aged man with a mustache has been spied roaming the premises. He's even wearing a brown top hat and brown suit under a white lab coat. He's most often seen on the curved stairway that connects the back of the shop to the second floor. There are those who say he has a habit of opening cabinets, throwing books, moving items, looking into bottles, rearranging locked displays, and setting off the alarms."

"How is he being punished if he's still getting to roam the place he loves so much?" I question.

"How do any of us know what punishment really is?" Emanual responds.

"I can think of ways to torture him," Sterling says. There's fire in his eyes as if he'd like to get his hands on the evil doctor.

"There are other ghosts spotted here as well so maybe they're getting their revenge. Two children have often been spotted inside and outside of the building."

"I'm done here," I say. "This history needs to be told so nothing like it can ever happen again, but it's not somewhere I want to be too long."

"Agreed," Sterling says. We walk from the building and stand in the street, waiting for the rest of our group. "Do you want to stop the tour?"

I smile up at him. I'm still feeling pain for the suffering that happened in that building, but I love that Sterling sees it and wants to make it better.

"I'd love to run away from history like this. I'd love to be ignorant to it, but if we don't learn from our past, how can we move forward to be better people? It might hurt me to hear about it, but my pain is nothing compared to what the people who were tortured at the hands of that evil man went through. I believe they are free now. I want to continue."

"You amaze me," Sterling says. The rest of our group comes out, everyone looking somber. We move on to our next destination.

"Why is that?"

"You don't run away from anything."

I laugh. I laugh hard for a moment. It feels good to feel humor when I've been feeling such despair only a few minutes before.

"Oh, Superman, if you only knew. I certainly run, but maybe someday I won't feel the need."

"Maybe I can help with that," he says with a wink.

"I sure hope so," I tell him honestly. I don't want to run, I just don't know any other way at this point in my life.

We next go to Jackson Square named after the legendary General Jackson who led the soldiers to victory during the Battle of New Orleans. We then stop at haunted houses and even stop for beers at some of the older establishments in town. Nothing touches me like the first stop though. They should probably end the tour with that one because it's all downhill after that.

I'm relieved when the tour is over and I'm very impressed when I see Sterling hand a hundred-dollar bill to our guide as a tip. He's done an amazing job and he deserves to be tipped well.

We're both a little melancholy as we head to Dooky Chase Restaurant, which opened its doors in 1941.

"I'm getting a full history lesson tonight." I smile at Sterling as we sit.

"I like to show off my city. I love it here," he says. "And this restaurant was *the* place for music, entertainment, civil rights meetings, and all culture in New Orleans."

"Well then I'm glad this is where you've brought me."

"Have I done good enough tonight to learn where you're from?" he asks.

I laugh, feeling the rest of my blues evaporating. "I have to admit I love your persistence." I'm not really answering him. The waiter appears and we order oysters Norman, crab cakes, gumbo, and duck. It's sure to all be delicious.

"Is that a no?" he pushes.

"That's a maybe soon."

"Why the mystery?" he asks.

I think about this seriously. "I've been lost for a long time. I had something happen three years ago that nearly ended my life, it was so painful. I don't want to talk about that, but there came a moment I had to decide if I wanted to move forward or not. My best friend assured me I *would* be moving forward. I'm trying to do just that." I pause as I take a sip of my drink.

"Each day that passes helps me climb from the pits I kept myself in for a very long time. I don't want to live in the past anymore. I want to live for today, and keep my eye on the future."

He reaches over and takes my hand. "I completely understand that," he tells me. "We all have shadows that lurk beside us. I'd like to know you better; I'd like to see you smile, laugh, and truly live." He leans back and winks. "And I'd like for you to love this city. Maybe you'll want to stick around for a while."

Our first course arrives as I gaze into the beautiful hazel eyes of the man who's becoming more and more important to me. We have a wonderful meal, and I let my guard down a little piece at a time as we get to know each other more with each passing minute. What does it all mean?

Maybe I'm not ready to know that just yet.

Chapter Eight

I'm exhausted. Seriously, I'm only twenty— How old am I again? I have to think for a moment since my real ID and my fake ID don't line up. I'm twenty-one. How can a bunch of middle school kids wear me out this badly? At least the last bell has rung, and the little demons are gone in the blink of an eye. It's Friday and I have the full weekend to recover.

"You appear to be very pensive about something."

I jump when Sterling's voice echoes in the empty gym. I look up and catch his eyes. He, of course, makes my heart start thundering. Why am I resisting him when he makes me feel this good? Will this feeling go away? How can I have this gut-clenching feeling with multiple men? What in the heck is wrong with me, dang it? Why can't I just settle down? Why can't I accept love?

"I'm tired," I finally say with a laugh.

He comes and sits next to me. "I get that. When I first began teaching, I seriously wondered how I'd survive each day. I'd go crawling home and pray for the weekend to start," he tells me.

"And now?" I could really use a pedicure. Maybe I'll treat myself to an extra, extra, *extra* long one. Can I get a four-hour foot massage? I don't know, but it's something worth asking for.

"Now, I look forward to school. I've followed these kids as they've moved on to high school, and I've been to multiple high school graduations. I take pride in the fact that I make learning fun for these students. Yes, we need to learn, but we also need to provide a good environment. For some of these kids, this is the only bright spot in their day. If school is torture, how can we expect them to grow?"

"I haven't thought about that before," I say, feeling a little selfish for my tiredness. "I do have some great students who seem to want to participate and truly enjoy being at school."

"They're all great. This is the time for them to be shaped into leaders of tomorrow," he tells me. "Some of them don't have a lot of positive role models in their lives so being here can make a difference in who they might become. It's our jobs to teach them, be an ear for them, and assure them they're incredible. It's their parents' job to guide them in other ways. It's hard not to cross that line at times, but I think we all do a pretty good job at this school."

"How much influence do we truly have over them, though?"

He laughs. "I don't know. I just know I'm doing my part in the best way I can. Come have a drink with me. It's Friday night and I need a vodka."

I laugh. "I was just thinking the same thing. I might be turning into an alcoholic," I say, only slightly worried.

"Just wait until finals, then we'll see what you're truly made of."

We leave the building and I climb in his truck. I don't have a vehicle. I don't like driving in cities and there's always public transportation wherever I might go, so there's no need to waste money on vehicles, insurance, and of course, the ever-climbing prices of fuel. I'd rather have the extra spending money. I'm trying to live on a teacher's salary, which isn't so easy to do. Every teacher in the nation deserves a raise, I decide.

We arrive at a nice bar. "I love bar food. It's a weakness of mine."

"Who doesn't love onion rings and fried cheese?" he asks.

"Ah, you're my kind of man."

There's a spark in his eyes that speaks right to me. We haven't discussed our marriage. I don't know what we really can say about it. It was impulsive and I'm not sure what we're going to do about it. I guess just keep moving forward like Stephy suggested.

We place our orders of junky, greasy, delicious food, and a couple of strong drinks, then sit back as we watch a band set up.

"Do you like live music?" he asks.

"We did meet for the first time at a jazz bar."

"That doesn't tell me if you like music."

"Yes, my tastes are ever changing. I used to only listen to country, but now I like jazz, soft rock, and I *really* love 80s bands."

"What's your favorite?"

I have to think for a minute. "I don't really have a favorite. I do love classic rock and anything that inspires emotions in me. It all depends on my mood." I lean in as if I'm embarrassed. "I have to admit I like some rap when I'm working out. It pumps me up."

He laughs. "I love that you're telling me that as if it's a dirty little secret."

"Well, it kind of is. I'm too old to be listening to Pump Up the Jam as if I'm fifteen."

"We're only as old as we want to be," he tells me. He winks. "I love Eminem and Beyoncé when I work out."

I laugh, completely shocked. "I somehow can't picture it. But Beyoncé is pretty damn hot so I can see how that motivates you to pump a little harder." I instantly blush as I realize the double entendre with that sentence. He joins me in laughter as a couple of platters of food are set on the table. This is only the appetizers. We might've ordered too much food. I feel as if I can eat an entire buffet at the moment though.

"I can't argue with that," he tells me. Then he smoothly adds more. "But she doesn't hold a candle to you."

This nearly makes me choke. "Oh, you're smooth, Superman. I'll take the lie and run with it, though." He doesn't argue. "I love to watch old videos when I'm doing cardio, like Janet Jackson's *If*, and anything by the Pussycat Dolls. Those women are as hot as hell. If anyone is in the room with me while I'm watching some of the videos I find myself blushing. The *If* video is way sexy."

"I haven't seen it but now I'm curious," he says. He moves to grab his phone. I reach out my hand and stop him.

"No way. You have to watch it when I'm not here."

"I'm not sure I can wait."

"I have faith in you that you can." We both take a couple of cheese sticks, dip them, and munch them down. "It's amazing how hungry I am by the end of the school day. I don't think I've ever eaten as much as I have this week."

"Yep, it takes a lot of calories to fuel our bodies to keep up with adolescent kids," he tells me. I'm eating my share and he's making me look as if I'm simply pecking at it. Maybe we haven't ordered too much.

"Does your family live here?"

"You've met my brother, who's now in wedded bliss. He just returned from a month-long honeymoon. He and his wife are tanned and looking at each other with googly eyes that are so disgusting it nearly makes me nauseous," he says with a big grin that counters his words. "I also have a little sister who's a pain in my butt. I love her to the moon and back."

"Do your parents live here?"

"Yep, but they've been on a traveling mission ever since my sister graduated high school five years ago. They're only here about three months of the year now. They've discovered Europe, and I fear they're going to eventually move there. They've been to Australia, Sweden, Italy, and on and on. They love cruises. They'll go on one, then go back to the countries they like the most on their stops for extended periods. They come home long enough to visit family, then they are off again."

"I think that's wonderful. I'd love if my parents traveled the world. They're still in my hometown, and they seem quite happy there. I don't know if they'll ever leave."

"What do they do?" he asks. I'm more relaxed as I sip on my Moscow Mule and eat my greasy food.

"My dad's a preacher and my mother owns a craft store. I can knit a bunny in my sleep," I tell him.

His eyes light up. "Your dad is a preacher?"

I laugh. "Yep, my entire life. I'm an only child. My mother always tells me I was such a great baby that she didn't want to risk having another. Then she adds that I was a terror for a few years before I came to my senses. I have pretty amazing parents."

"It sounds like you miss them."

"I do, but I talk to my mom a few times a week and she loves that I'm out exploring, even if I haven't left the US yet. She tells me I need to live it up." I don't tell Sterling that my mother doesn't know I'm a teacher right now. She still thinks I'm working for a bank. I can't exactly tell her I'm reinventing myself every year. It's hard for me to keep anything from her, but so far I haven't slipped.

"What's the most fun thing you've ever done?" I don't want to keep the focus on me for too long.

He sits back as he thinks about his answer. "When my brother and I were young we were a pair of heathens. My parents have a big property in the country, and we raised all kinds of different animals through the years. They wanted us to know how to live off the land. We'd fail with a lot of animals, but my favorite was when we had cows. My brother and I would get into cow poop fights. We'd come back to the house covered in the stuff and my mother would make us hose down and strip before we were allowed to go inside."

I wrinkle my nose at him. "That's your idea of fun?" I gasp.

"Why not?" he says, completely relaxed.

"I grew up in a small town and my bestie owns a huge ranch with lots of cows. There wasn't a single time I ever thought it would be fun to sling poop on her or have it thrown at me."

He laughs hard at that. "I'm not surprised. I'm sure you've never rolled around in the mud either."

I give him an indignant look. "Now, *that's* where you'd be wrong."

"Oh, really. Correct me then," he demands.

"I wasn't great at sports but I'd play sometimes. We were having a weekend softball game, just a bunch of kids from school gathered together. I wasn't that good at anything that had to do with a ball, but I liked playing if it wasn't done as a team sport where it mattered how I played. It suddenly started pouring rain and the field turned into a giant mud pit. Several of the kids ran off, but the majority of us continued playing. It ended up being the most fun game I've ever played. We were sliding into the bases, into each other, and even into the fence, and all of us were covered from head to toe in mud, bruises, and a few scrapes." I stop and have a sip of my drink. "I had to be hosed off before I was allowed to enter the house, but at least I didn't smell like manure."

"How do you know a million cats hadn't already pooped in that dirt?" he questions, horrifying me. "I'd rather have cow dung all over me than cat poop."

A shudder runs through me. This was never a thought I'd considered. I decide I'd better change the subject really quick or I'm going to lose my appetite, and the food is too dang good for that to happen.

"Have you broken any bones?"

He laughs again. "Okay, I'll let you change the subject," he tells me. I smile gratefully at him. "I've broken my arm, but I haven't had any major injuries since I was twelve so I count that as a win."

We continue to chat for the next three hours. We finish our food and I have a few more drinks while he switches over to water. We stay long enough for the band to begin, and then it gets too noisy for us to talk anymore. We finally get up and leave.

I realize I'm not ready for the date to end. It's been easy and fun, and I've gotten to know more about Sterling. I'm thinking of him with his real name. I like him as Superman. I like him as Clark Kent. But I *really* like him as Sterling Worth.

He leads me to his truck and holds the door open. His arm brushes against me as he waits for me to climb inside. I feel flutters in my stomach. My desire for him is growing. I like it — I like it a lot. What will I do about it? Can I be that woman who's so forward she takes what she wants? Not yet, but maybe I can grow into her.

We continue chatting on the drive back to my place and he parks. We both sit here for a second, and I'm wondering what I should do. Should I invite him inside? I have no doubt what will happen if I do that. Am I ready? I think I am.

He exits the truck and I find myself short of breath. I can't seem to find the words to ask him inside. He opens my door and I can see fire burning in his gaze. He says nothing as he places a hand on my back and walks me up the sidewalk to my front door. We both stop.

"I've had an incredible evening," he says. We're face to face, extremely close to each other. He lifts a hand and brushes the hair from my face. A shiver runs through me as his finger lingers on my ear for a moment. My heart skips a beat and I gaze at him, feeling shaky.

"I've enjoyed it a lot," I say, my voice husky.

"What are we to do about our situation?" he asks. He moves just a little closer.

"I don't know. I've been trying to figure it out." I want to invite him in. I want him to wrap his arms around me and take away the confusion. I want the choice taken from me.

"We have plenty of time to figure it all out," he assures me.

He stops talking as he wraps his arms around me and tugs. I press against him. Finally! The kiss I've been waiting for is finally going to happen. My heart races and my skin heats. I like being in his arms. I like him.

I can't explain the heat between us. I can't explain the connection, the feeling that we know each other even though we're still strangers. I can't explain any of it, but I feel it all. We're attracted to each other, and we're becoming friends. Can it lead to more? Why not? Why can't it?

His head descends, and his lips gently touch mine. He's kissing me as if he isn't in a hurry. He's cherishing me, building the flames higher in my body. Just a light brushing of lips. I sigh against him as I push closer, needing him to quench the fire he's building inside of me.

He groans against my mouth and then clutches me tighter, his tongue slipping inside. The gentleness of only seconds before is gone as he tugs me closer, his fingers squeezing my hips. I feel as if he can utterly consume me. I want him to. I want to feel alive and cherished. I want to feel desired and wanted. I need him.

I reach up and run my fingers through his hair. I gasp for air when his lips retreat, then fall into him again as he deepens our kiss. I'm losing myself in him just as I had the first time we shared a kiss. There's magic between us. Maybe it's this city full of voodoo and mystery. Maybe it's the man himself, and maybe it's me that's ever changing.

I can't breathe . . .

Fear begins to creep in. I don't want another person to have this power over me. I don't want to let go. This hunger between us is all-consuming, and it's scary. I'm not sure what to think about it.

I must tense because he pulls back. He separates our bodies as he reaches up and cups my cheek. His gaze holds me captive. I can't pull back. I'm at his mercy even if that frightens me.

"Thank you for another wonderful night, Mrs. Worth," he whispers. The name sends a shudder down my spine. It's a gentle reminder that I'm already his. He lets me go, though, letting me know he's willing to wait; he's willing to give me the time I need to adjust to all of this.

I'm completely off balance.

"Thank you for a wonderful night." I need to explain myself, but he stops me by holding a finger to my lips.

"Give it time," he says. "I have a feeling all we need is a little more time."

I pause for several heartbeats. "Can you read my mind?" I'm only half kidding. He takes a step back from me, his finger falling away, and I lick my lips. His gaze focuses on the motion and a shudder passes through him. He takes another step back. He grins at me, a big, huge, Cheshire cat grin.

"If I could read women's minds, I'd rule the world," he tells me. "I can read your body, though. I want you. You want me. But you're not quite ready. We'll come together again, and we're going to make fireworks burst when it happens," he assures me.

"You might just be right."

He steps a few more feet away. "I'm going to run away before I drag you inside. You turn me on beyond my wildest fantasies, Charlie. I'm going to make you beg to come to my bed again." This finally makes me smile.

"Oh really?" I'm half tempted to follow after him as he pulls farther away. What is wrong with me that I want to run until someone is pulling away, then I want to chase.

"Yes, really," he assures me. "I'm a very patient man when it comes to a woman as unique and amazing as you."

He doesn't let me answer him. He turns and jogs to his truck. I laugh as he guns the motor and drives away. I sort of love living this way. I love that it's unpredictable and magical and beautiful. I go into my house and shut the door, wondering if I'm in a dream and none of this is actually happening.

I grab a bottle of wine and my phone. Of course, I need to call Stephy. I want to hear her tell me to have sex with my husband. I need to have someone tell me it's okay. It doesn't matter if I'm a consenting adult. It doesn't even matter if we've already slept together. It only matters that I feel good about myself when I wake up in the morning.

I dial her.

"Hello, beautiful," she answers with a giggle. I can hear music in the background.

"Tell me I'm a fool to let this man get away from me . . ."

She laughs. "You're a fool!"

"Why do I want to run to him one minute, then away the next?" I take a gulp of wine.

"Oh, darling, because you're a woman. Don't you realize we're all a little crazy?"

Now, I'm laughing with her. "Then why in the world do men want to be with us?"

"Because we make the world go round," she says. "It's the yin and yang . . . and the bang."

I gasp then burst out laughing. Stephy loves to make shocking statements. I know who she truly is. I love that the rest of the world doesn't. She only lets so many people in. The rest believe the image she shows has no flaws. I *know* the girl who plays in the mud. I've certainly made the right call. Maybe I should call Superman back to my house. I take another gulp of wine. Nope. I'll wait. I'll see what comes next . . .

Chapter Nine

"Court's dismissed."

These are my favorite new words. It's emotionally draining to go back in time and think about my past. I've loved all of it. Some I miss, some I don't, but I've enjoyed every moment. Stephy's in my corner for the moments I feel bad about myself. She reminds me that I'm living life to the fullest and I have nothing to feel shame over.

We silently walk from the courtroom. Normally, Cash and Stephy are chatterboxes as we exit, but this evening they are quiet. We climb into the SUV that transports us back to the hotel. Why am I so melancholy? I have nothing to be sad about. I'm with my loved ones and I'm remembering a past that is both broken and beautiful.

Cash has some calls to make so he leaves Stephy and me alone in our suite. We head out to the balcony with our wine glasses in hand. I hear someone call from below and look down to see a couple in the pool. She's giggling as she wraps herself in his arms, and then the two of them share a hot kiss that immediately takes me back in time. I close my eyes and dive into the past once more . . .

My stomach is tingling as I ride beside Sterling to his home. It's been two weeks since I found him again at the school, two wonderful, exciting, *frustrating* weeks. We've flirted, gone on dates, shared a few kisses, and sought each other out at school . . . and then we've gone our separate ways.

Not tonight.

We just finished dinner and he asked me if I wanted to see his home. I knew immediately what he was really asking me. I'm ready. I nodded, unable to find words. And now we're in his big truck and we've just turned off the main road and are driving down a tree-lined drive. When we come into view of the house I gasp. It isn't what I've been expecting.

"This is your home?"

"Don't be too impressed," he tells me with a chuckle. "I bought it ten years ago for a heck of a deal, and I've been working on it ever since. Let me promise you that anything that can go wrong in an old house will go wrong."

He might be telling me not to be impressed, but the place is huge. It's an old Southern mansion. I can see it's a work in progress, but the two-story house with a wrap-around deck on both stories is magnificent. It's certainly more home than one man needs. It has to be over five thousand square feet.

He pulls up to the front porch and jumps from the truck, then comes around and opens my door. I love what a gentleman he is. The house is fitting for a Southern man. He takes my hand, leads me up the steps, and opens the door. I'm surprised it isn't locked.

"There's not much crime in this area. I can never find my house keys anyway," he says.

The entryway is large and there's a double curved staircase that leads to the second floor. I want to look around, but I'm also nervous and unsure of where I stand with this husband of mine. It's so odd to think we're married. I don't feel married at all. We don't live together, and we've only had sex one time. It isn't anything like my marriage to Bentley. It's not even like the brief marriage I shared with Warren. But it is unique.

It's a bit humid today and it seems he doesn't have air conditioning. It must be miserable in the middle of summer. He doesn't seem to mind. He's probably adjusted to it over the years. I've always wondered how people can live in constant humidity. I guess if you're born and raised in it, it's not a problem.

"Let's get a drink then take a swim," Sterling says. We move into a huge kitchen that he's obviously updated. He reaches into the fridge, grabs a bottle of wine, then takes two glasses from the cupboard. Within seconds he has the top off and sweet wine poured for both of us. He hands me mine.

"I don't have a swimsuit."

His eyes gleam. "Good. Neither do I. Too constricting when I want to be free."

My stomach does summersaults. I can tell him no right now without fear that he'll be upset with me. He's a gentleman through and through. There's nothing in me that wants to deny him or myself — not anymore. I know this isn't about a swim, this is about us coming back together. It's long past time.

"Let's take a swim," I say slightly breathless.

We move out his back door and I'm once again impressed. He has a large crystal-clear pool with a winding waterfall streaming into it, stirring up the water, and making it seem quite magical. Furniture and plants are scattered around, making it nicer than many resorts I've been to.

"I'm very impressed."

"I don't like being indoors. I worked on the pool before anything else on this nonstop project. It took me two years to get it just how I want, but now it's minimal maintenance. I swim nightly," he says. He sets our wine bottle on a table, then grabs my glass and sets it aside. He steps back and begins undressing. I find myself frozen as I stare at him.

He's not shy. It only takes him seconds to remove all of his clothes. My eyes worship his beautiful body, and I notice right away that he's hard. Damn, he's beautiful from head to toe. My eyes finally meet his again and I see heat in his expression. Before it gets too intense he winks at me, turns, and dives into the water. I watch the fluid motion of his perfect body slicing through the water. I freeze to the spot.

He swims for about five minutes and then props himself up on a raised section right by the waterfall, beads of water splashing over him. He looks as if he should be on the cover of every magazine in the supermarket. If I saw his image, hard and wet, I'd buy all of the copies.

"Are you going to join me?" he asks, a wicked grin on his sexy full lips.

I shake myself out of my fog. I nod, unable to find my voice. My fingers tremble as I begin unbuttoning my dress. I get enough undone to drop it to my feet. I step out of it, then kick off my low-slung heels. I stand for another moment deciding if I'm going to strip completely. It makes me feel incredibly vulnerable to take everything off.

He's seen my naked body before. The reality is that I want nothing between us. I want him to slide inside of me, and I want it to happen fast. It's been a very long time. I drop the rest of my clothes then dive into the water. It's cooler than I expected, and I come out of the water with a bit of a gasp. I look up and find Sterling looking straight at me. The fire in his eyes is a beacon.

"You look like a siren on the rock. I thought that was my job," I say, my voice breathless, my body on fire in the cool water.

"I knew from the moment I saw you that you were utter trouble," he quickly replies. "I can see you as a siren enticing pirates into the rocks." He pauses for a while before adding more. "Have I told you how much I love trouble?"

I laugh as I lazily swim closer to him. He hasn't moved. I can't see his lower body beneath the water, and I'm hungry to get a glimpse of him again . . . hard, pulsing, and his body mine, and only mine . . . for now.

"Nope. You told me you don't like trouble at all," I remind him. "As a matter of fact, you panicked the night I met you at the bar."

"I'm a changed man," he says.

"I think we're both changed." I'm getting closer. I give him my best smile before I dive below the surface to cool myself off. I feel like the siren I accused him of being. Maybe I should sing him a song and lead him my way.

Coming up for air, I'm right in front of him. He looks sexy as hell and as if he's barely holding on to control. I like him this way. I climb onto the ledge with him. The air hits my nipples making them hard and tingly. The look in his eyes is unmistakable. It's taking all of his restraint not to plunge straight inside of me. Knowing this makes me bolder and more confident.

Neither of us speak as we sit inches apart, both of our eyes trailing over one another. It's been a month and a half since I've last had him inside my body, and yet it feels like ages longer. I never knew I could be such a nymphomaniac but I'm not unhappy about it. I like the desires flooding me, and I don't know if I can ever go back to who I was. I don't want to.

"I'm loving this pool more and more the longer I'm here." My words are barely audible over the sound of the waterfall splashing beside us.

"I'm loving it a hell of a lot more with you in it," he tells me. I briefly wonder if this scene has played out for him before. I quickly push that thought aside. It's none of my business and I'm not going to do or say anything that's going to ruin this perfect moment.

"You are so damn sexy, Superman." I like reverting to his nickname. It seems the more turned on I am, the more I think of him as a superhero.

He smiles as he leans forward, running his hand across my chest. Chills rush down my spine and through my body at his light touch across my aching nipple.

"I'm going to touch and taste you all over," he promises me. I don't want to argue with that. I want to taste him too, but right now I'm barely holding myself up as we gaze at each other.

He runs those magical fingers across my chest, down my stomach and over my hips before circling my back and pulling me closer . . . but not close enough. I reach out and touch his thigh, feeling a quiver beneath my touch. We're both on the edge of control and I think we each love it.

Sterling finally pulls me close and kisses me, his lips molding to mine. I sigh against his mouth then willingly open to him. Each time his lips take mine it's like the first. Each time his tongue slips inside my mouth, I want to pull him in farther. I can't get close enough to his rock-hard body, and his magical tongue and fingers . . . and thick, strong, beautiful shaft.

He grabs me and pulls us up on the side of the pool and lies over me, his hardness pressing against my softness. It's yin and yang, and it's never been more beautiful. I love how we fit together. I also don't want this to end too quickly.

I somehow manage to turn us, break our lips apart, and run my tongue down his neck. I suck on his salty skin before kissing my way down until I reach a nipple. I lick and suck one and then the other while my hands slide over his beautiful abs.

I begin to move down his body, and he reaches into my hair and tries to tug me away. I don't let him. I need to taste him. I slide down his solid abs, then take his manhood in my hand. I stroke it up and down for a moment as he groans, then I reach out and swipe my tongue across the head of him. Beautiful. Tasty. Thick. Solid. He's mine . . . at least he's mine right now.

I finally suck him deep, and he cries out as I squeeze my fingers around his shaft and suck him in and out of my mouth. He's pulsing as I twist my tongue over his head, sucking soft then hard.

"Enough," he cries, his grip on my hair tight as he tugs me off of him. Before I can protest he turns us, then traps my hands at my sides. He's above me, a fierce warrior with nearly black eyes he's so turned on. I love that I've done this to him.

He doesn't kiss me this time. He simply moves down my body, kissing his way between my breasts. He shoves my thighs apart then makes me scream when his tongue runs the length of my slit. He stops and sucks my clit, making my back arch off of the rock. This is even greater than I remember. Why have we waited so long to do this again?

I grow hotter and my clit more sensitive. He keeps teasing it, licking and sucking until I'm a mess beneath him. I can't stop the moans escaping me and I'm praying his neighbors live miles away because I'm sure the sound will easily carry in the warm night air.

He swipes his tongue again, and I lose control. My legs shake, my core pulses as he keeps licking, his touch gentling, his warm air blowing over my sensitive flesh.

He draws out my orgasm until I'm a puddle beneath him. I can't move. I can't breathe. I can't think. I'm limp as I fall back against the rock. Heaven. I feel as if I've been touched by heaven.

"Someone needs to cool off," he tells me.

"What?" I'm too hazy to comprehend what he's saying or doing.

I come out of my haze quickly when he lifts me and jumps into the pool. The cold water on my hot flesh is a definite wake-up call. We emerge from the water and I gasp at him, utterly shocked he'd do this.

"I'm going to hurt you," I say as I cling to his hot body.

"Promises, promises," he tells me, making me tingle all over again. It's insane how quickly he can rev me back up after such an intense orgasm.

He pushes me against the wall of the pool and begins kissing me, but rips his mouth away as he traces his tongue across my throat, sucking where my pulse is beating out of control. He moves down and worships my breasts, kneading and sucking and licking until I nearly come again. I want to touch him, but he's making me so weak I can't do anything other than focus on the pleasure he's bringing me.

"Please, Sterling, please." This teasing is killing me. I need him to fill me up now. I need him to give us both pleasure.

"Yes," he tells me. He moves us back to the ledge and sets me down, the height perfect for our bodies to align. He pulls me to the edge, grips my hips tight, then thrusts himself forward. I scream. He's so perfect, our bodies a natural fit. I wrap my arms around his neck as he squeezes my ass and pumps in and out. I bite down on his shoulder and moan as he builds me higher and higher.

I want more. I want it all.

As if he's reading my mind, he pumps harder, faster, both of us losing control. His fingers are squeezing my flesh, and I don't care. I dig my teeth into his shoulder as shudders rack my body. I let him go, throw my head back, and scream as pulse after pulse rushes through me. I feel his heat as he cries out, his release filling me.

It's several moments before his body relaxes and he leans against me, both of us holding on tight to one another. We're panting, no longer feeling a trace of cold.

This moment is perfect, it's unique, and it's beautiful. I don't want to ever let him go. I'm not sure how long I'll feel this way and that thought breaks my heart a little.

We stay like this for a long time without speaking. Finally, he leans back. He smiles at me before moving forward and gently kissing my lips.

"Stay," he says.

"Yes," I tell him. There's not any part of me that wants to go anywhere — not tonight at least.

He cradles me in his arms then walks the two of us out of the pool. He sets me down by a little hut I hadn't noticed when we first came out. He wraps me in a towel and then we go to the loungers with our wine and cuddle together as we sip wine, look at the stars, and get to know a bit more about each other. I'm falling for Sterling . . . I'm just not sure how far this fall will take me.

Chapter Ten

It's been a week since Sterling and I made love in his pool. He asked me to stay and I haven't left. I keep telling myself this isn't my home, but I can't get myself to leave. We drive to school together, we come back to his place, make dinner, swim, and make love . . . sometimes not in that order.

As long as the two of us don't mention the future we get to live in this beautiful paradise. I like his place; I like this moment. I like not having all of the answers. I don't want all of the answers. I want to be free and live happy. I want to smile often and laugh every single day.

"Ms. Sapphire, are you listening?"

I shake my head and look up. My student Billy is gazing at me with his big blue eyes. He's my favorite in the class. For all of those teachers who say they don't have a favorite, they are liars. We all do. Billy is mine. He has this crooked little smile and bright red hair. He's a devil and an angel all in one. I will truly miss him when

New Orleans is no longer my home — and I know it won't be forever.

"I'm sorry, Billy, I must've been off in the universe somewhere."

He laughs. "You're always off in space," he tells me. I probably am.

"Mr. Worth is doing a cool science fair in the front lot. Can we go . . . please?" he asks, practically jumping up and down in front of me.

"What do you mean?"

"Jimmy said that right after lunch, Mr. Worth is taking them outside and blowing things up. I want to go really bad," Billy repeats.

"Me too," several of my other students demand. I'm not sure I'm allowed to deviate from my schedule. I *am* the teacher though, and I kind of want to see things explode. I know Sterling knows how to make things burn . . . he made my body tingle multiple times the night before *and* this morning.

"I guess we can go and see what's happening."

"Yahoo!" Billy rushes to the door.

"Stop!" He barely contains himself from flinging open the door and rushing through it. "Let's do this in an orderly way, and I want the promise of each and every one of you to not make a sound in the hallway. I don't want to get into trouble with the principal."

Several of my students giggle as I move to the doorway. "I want you to make lines of two across and quietly follow me. If we don't do this right, we won't get to do it again," I warn them.

"We'll be super good," Billy promises. There's also a wicked twinkle in his eyes that tells me he might have a hard time keeping that promise.

"Okay, let's go." They cheer until I give them a stern look. I'm getting a bit too good at the teacher look. But they go silent. I open the door and we make our way down the hallway without a sound. That all changes as soon as we're through the front door and we see half the school standing outside as Sterling stands in the middle of it all. Why didn't he tell me he was doing this? I'm going to have to ask him later.

"Well, it looks like we're getting more and more kids," Sterling says.

"Yeah! Can we please start now?" one of his students asks.

"I don't see why not," Sterling says with a big smile. "Let's blow some things to smithereens." He pauses. "All in the name of science. And just remember to never, ever, ever, *ever* do this alone, with friends, or without a teacher or your parents right beside you," he adds.

"What if it's our job to blow things up?" one student asks.

"Well then, you'll be an adult, and hopefully you'll know what you're doing because of this class," Sterling says with another chuckle. I'm sure at least one of these kids will be a building demolisher or work in the military, or do any number of other jobs that they get to blow up things. Maybe more than one after this fun lesson.

"Okay, it's time for Sterling Worth, Scientist Extraordinaire to start the magic," Sterling says, making the kids cheer again. It's not that difficult to get them excited. I love it. I love this school. I love how engaged the teachers are and how much they love their students.

"I'm going to need some help," he says, and all of the kids raise their hands and eagerly jump up and down in the air.

"Leo, you can be my assistant." I smile as Leo walks up to Sterling.

He's another of my favorites even though I don't have him in my class. He's so dang shy, but he's been opening up more and more. His dad plays football and is gone a lot, and his mother is about the greatest woman on the planet. He has the smoothest dark skin I've ever seen, and medium length hair that's always a mess. He'll sometimes be playing with his pencil and wedge it into his hair, then forget all about it. I think he'll have a heck of a growth spurt and be able to bench press any of the teachers in this school by the time he graduates.

"What do I get to do, Mr. Worth?" he asks.

"Our first project is to make a rocket with nothing more than Mentos and Diet Coke," Sterling says with a wide grin.

Leo's eyes widen before he shakes his head. "I don't see how you're going to make that happen," he says.

"Well, you will soon find out. This is the same kind of technology that sends rockets into space," Sterling says. "It's pretty dang great. I've created this spinning cage so we can do it quickly. I have a funnel in the soda bottle. I want you to drop the mints into it then quickly run back while I flip the bottle upside down. Are you ready?" he asks as he hands about eight white mints to Leo.

"I'm ready," he says, his voice growing more excited.

"Good. On the count of one. Three . . . two . . . one!" Leo tosses the mints into the funnel, then quickly jumps back as the soda immediately begins to fizzle. Sterling quickly flips the soda bottle upside down and the mints do their job and cause a forceful geyser of soda which shoots the bottle about eight feet into the air. The kids all around gasp.

"Again, again," someone demands. "That's the coolest thing I've ever seen."

Sterling laughs. "Oh, the day's just beginning," he promises his students. "We have a ways to go yet. The reason this works is that the candy reacts with the carbonation in the soda to release a gas that builds up pressure in the bottle. When the pressure becomes too great, the gas spurts out of the bottle and carries some of the soda with it in the form of a geyser. This shows all of you that when there is too much pressure inside something, it has to escape."

"Why?" a kid asks.

He gives a wicked grin. "Let me use an example we can all relate to," he says before laughing. I'm curious. That's one evil grin he's wearing.

"Who of you farts?" I'm not standing close to him, and I feel my cheeks instantly heat. I can't believe he's just said this. I look around as the girls are giggling and the boys are outright laughing and jumping in the air with their hands held high.

"My sister says there's something wrong with me because I fart too much," Billy says.

"My mom says she's gonna make me sleep on the porch cause my farts are so stinky," Leo says, making all of the kids giggle even louder.

"What happens if there's a build-up in your stomach and you don't fart?" Sterling asks.

"My belly hurts," a kid says. "Mom says it's rude to fart, but then my tummy hurts, and I think *that's* rude."

"Well, farting is caused by gas in the bowels. Ordinarily the intestines produce up to two thousand milliliters of gas each and every day, which is then passed from us at regular intervals. These gases are methane, nitrogen, and carbon dioxide. The smells depend on the ratio of gases and what foods you've consumed."

"We have methane in us? I thought that's used for driving," Leo says.

"Well, it's primarily used as fuel, so you're partially right. We use it to make heat and light. It's also used to manufacture organic chemicals. Methane can be formed by the decay of natural materials and is common in landfills, marshes, septic systems and . . . sewers. It can form an explosive mixture in air levels as low as five percent."

"We can explode?" a girl cries out.

"Nope. We aren't going to explode because we all pass gas," Sterling says with another big smile.

"Nope. I don't fart," a girl says with her hands on her hips.

"You do too. Everyone farts. Girls just don't admit it," Billy says.

"You can't prove it," the girl tells him, looking very self-righteous. I'm still blushing, but I decide not to weigh in on the fart topic. I'm slightly mortified. Why does talking about farting embarrass me so much as an adult? I don't care. There are some things I refuse to speak of.

"Okay, back to our lesson. Farting is generated by swallowed air, digestion, high-fiber foods, and the by-products of intestinal bacteria. Some disorders can cause excess gas. Though passing wind is normal, it does embarrass a lot of people. But if we couldn't expel these gases, it would be much worse."

"Why?" a kid asks.

"Because then we might explode like the soda bottle," Sterling says. There's a gasp in the audience. I need to do my research. I wonder if that's true. I have no idea.

"Well why does it have to stink so much?" a kid asks. That makes all of the other kids laugh even harder.

"That all depends on the person. If you're eating certain foods they process differently, causing bad smells."

"I don't like farting," a kid calls out.

"Well, it's better than our bodies launching up into the air as high as our soda bottle," Sterling tells his rapt audience. There are several nods of agreement with him on that one.

"Okay, let's move on to the next experiment," he says. I want to wipe my brow in relief. I'm done with the fart conversation. "The next is liquid fireworks."

The kids are immediately distracted as they begin jumping up and down as a couple of teachers bring the next items to the table.

"You can create your own simulated fireworks without danger or a messy explosion," he says.

"Boo. I like messy and danger," a kid calls out.

"We all think we like that until someone loses a finger," Sterling says.

"That wouldn't be very fun," a kid says.

"Unless it was really cool," Billy says. Yep, this kid is definitely going to blow things up when he gets older.

"We're doing this experiment so you can learn all about diffusion, which is the gradual mixing of two or more substances. Some things are meant to go together like peanut butter and jelly, and some things aren't meant to ever touch," he says as he moves to the table where a jar has been placed.

"I'm going to fill this jar about two-thirds full of water," he says as he does just that. "Now, I need another volunteer." Hands shoot into the air. "Lily, it's your turn." Lily is a champ. This girl will do anything at any time. I believe she can truly rule the school with evil or good if she wants. She's a natural leader and isn't afraid of anything.

"I need you to add two tablespoons of oil into this bowl," he says. She grabs the measuring spoon and adds the oil. "Now, choose one of the colors of food coloring and put ten drops of it into the oil." She chooses green and carefully adds her drops. "Perfect, now I want you to dump the oil mixture into the water."

"Do I go fast or slow?" she asks. I love what a perfectionist she is.

"Just pour it in normally," he says. She steps over and dumps the mixture into the water. "Now, move over here and we'll fill a few more bottles so everyone has a chance to see."

She moves over and they do this a few more times. Pretty soon little mini-fireworks are going off in the oil-water mixture.

"How's that happening?" a kid asks in awe.

"This happens as the food coloring separates from the oil and diffuses into the water," Sterling says. "You want to always have a parent with you at all times when doing any kind of experiment but this one is pretty safe for even younger kids, and it's pretty dang cool to watch," Sterling finishes.

The kids move on and do a few more experiments. By the time he reaches the end, the entire school is surrounding Sterling and his helpers. I'm just as fascinated at the kids are. If my science classes had been this cool in school I might've enjoyed them a lot more.

"The final experiment for the day is a baking soda explosion," Sterling tells the kids.

"We're going to have Jimmy put three teaspoons of baking soda in the middle of this tissue and twist the ends of it so it looks like a little pocket. Then Mallory is going to put a fourth cup of warm water into a Ziplock plastic bag and add a half cup of vinegar to it." He stops as his students perform their tasks.

"Okay, Jimmy, drop the tissue into the plastic bag and I'll quickly zip it closed," he says. Jimmy drops the tissue and Sterling seals the bag. Everyone watches as the tissue dissolves, releasing the baking soda into the water-vinegar mixture. It instantly reacts.

"This is creating carbon dioxide. The gas is expanding right now. The bag is inflating."

We all watch as the bag gets bigger and bigger until, boom! The bag explodes in a small but very impressive explosion.

"Wow!" several kids call out. "Do it again. Do it again."

Sterling laughs. "You've all been good sports today and we'll talk more about this in class tomorrow. I want you all to raise your hands high and promise to not do any of these experiments without your parents right next to you," he finishes.

"No way," a couple of the kids say. Sterling gives them stern looks. They look down but I notice not many of the kids are making any promises.

"Class is dismissed. See you all tomorrow," Sterling tells them.

It looks like a stampede as the kids rush toward the school as the ending bell rings. They have to grab their coats and bags and get to their buses or their awaiting parents. I move over to Sterling.

"This was incredibly cool, but I can see how it might go wrong once they get home."

He laughs. "That's why we left a voicemail, email, and sent a note home in each kid's backpack of what we were doing today. The parents can now threaten them for no science experiments without parental supervision."

"You've thought of it all."

"That's because I was a wild child and I'd be rushing in the door to try each of these over again at their age. Of course, I also went into science in school because I was fascinated by it all from a very young age," he says with a shrug.

"I hated science in school." I pause and give him a wink. "If you'd have been my teacher I think I would've changed my mind."

"Are you flirting with me, Mrs. Worth?" he asks.

I laugh. "I think I am." I'm truly enjoying this husband of mine.

"Then I'd better see if I can do something about that. Let's go make some explosions of our own . . . with zero students around."

"I think that's the best experiment you've planned all day," I tell him.

We walk arm in arm from the school. There's no reason to hide it anymore. We're together . . . but for how long?

Chapter Eleven

Stephy lifts her glass in the air as people around us chat, drink, laugh, and sing. It's a Friday night and the band is about to begin. It's been too long since I've seen her. She's determined to have me do this on my own, but I disagree with her.

I think I can find myself while still being with her. She'll figure it out. Maybe it's more about her, maybe she needs the separation in order to find herself. Maybe we're both broken, and I just haven't realized that yet.

"Hold your glass up," Stephy demands.

"To what?"

She leans closer. "For your *real* birthday." I'm sort of shocked to hear the words. I was beyond thrilled when she called a few days earlier telling me she's coming for a visit. I hadn't even thought about my birthday coming up. We've always celebrated together, and we always make promises and vows for the next year.

"I completely forgot," I say as I hold my glass in the air.

She laughs. "You never have been a fan of your birthday. I would totally get that if we were in our sixties, but being that we're in our twenties that's just criminal," she tells me. She loves any excuse to celebrate at any time.

"I have so many new birthdays I can't keep track of any of them," I tell her. "Do you realize I've been here for six months? How in the world has that happened? It's a great place, but it's still not home."

I'm shocked as I say the words. Life's become normal for me in New Orleans. I've been living with Sterling for months, and it's been good, it's been *really* good . . . but something is missing, something is off. Something keeps me from thinking of this place as home.

"You're growing restless again, aren't you?" Stephy asks, seeming a little bummed.

"I don't know," I admit. "I'm not really sure how in the heck I'm feeling. If I could figure that out, I'd be a much happier person."

We stand up and move to the balcony where people are partying. It's always a party in New Orleans. I've grown bored with this too. Maybe I want the country again. Maybe I want the peacefulness and quiet. Maybe my mother has been right all along. That's slightly horrifying.

"Look up at the stars," she says. I look up and see nothing. I just turn to her and raise a brow. "Just because we can't see them beneath the bright city lights doesn't mean they aren't there," she says.

"It's easy to stop believing when something is out of sight. I love that you always believe though, no matter what."

"Well, you know I simply want the best for you in life, at all times, and in all things. I think New Orleans is wonderful, but I also think you're starting to lose yourself again."

I think about her words. "I don't understand it. I don't know what's wrong with me. I like it here. I love my job. I love Sterling." I stop. We use the word *love* so dang easily. I'm quite aware of that fact and yet I still do it. If the word was used more reverently then maybe it would still have its true meaning.

"You just don't love him enough," Stephy says with a sigh. She gives me a smile. "I know the feeling. I want to find my prince, but all I seem to locate are frogs."

I laugh. "If you keep kissing them one might turn into your king and worship you for the rest of your life, as he should," I tell her.

"I tell myself that all the time," she says. "But you know, Charlie, you have to live in the world first to truly appreciate it. Maybe you're losing yourself because you're hiding. Maybe you aren't actually living in the world, maybe you're just existing."

"How am I hiding? I go to school five days a week, I'm with Sterling seven nights a week, and we date, and do things together all of the time."

"Are you doing things *for* him, or because *you* want to do them?"

I have to think about this. "I honestly don't know. But I do know I laugh a lot when I'm with him and yet I can still come home and feel utterly empty."

"Oh, Char, I'm not sure what to say," she says after a few heartbeats.

"It's going to end, isn't it?" I'm heartbroken.

She grabs my hand. "That's not necessarily true." I don't know if she's trying to convince me or herself. I don't know if she wants me to have eternal love more than I do. She probably does. I don't get why. She's the only person in the world who knows what I had with Bentley. She's the only one who knows how much I still love him to this day.

"I can share my body. I can take pleasure in a man, and I have. But to give my heart seems an impossible task. It seems the ultimate betrayal. I only have so much of myself I'm able to give."

She sighs. "Because you gave everything to Bentley." It's not a question.

"Yes, yes, I did." I pause to think. "How horrible am I to tease these men, to be with them when I know I won't stay in the end?" I'm feeling like a monster.

"Are you with them to hurt them?" she asks.

"Of course not." I gasp. I can't comprehend being so horrible.

"Do you want to stay forever?" I tense at her words.

"I want to *want* to stay forever."

"But you don't think there's anyone out there who can make you feel that's what you want?" she asks.

"No, I honestly don't. I truly loved Warren . . . until I woke up from my coma. Once I did, I realized I loved him, but not enough. I don't know if I'm capable of loving deeply again, not after Bentley."

"You know I love you to the moon and back, and Bentley's my twin. Losing him ripped me up too. I know him, Char, I know him more than anyone else other than you. He'd be dying right now if he knew you'd go through life alone."

I feel tears in my eyes. "I'm not alone, though."

"You can be in a room full of people and still be alone," she points out. "You are vibrant, beautiful, and funny. You can be with anyone you want. You just have to decide that's what you really want."

"This is getting far too deep. I'm so tired of crying." I wipe a tear away, then put on a sassy expression. "You do realize I'm more than just a pretty face, right?"

She laughs hard. "Thatta girl!" She holds her hand up and gets us more drinks. "Here's to brilliant, beautiful women who rule the world."

"I'll certainly toast to that." I clink glasses with her.

"Now, we have a rule that we make resolutions every birthday, so what's yours going to be this next year of your life?" she asks.

"I haven't thought about it." We normally think seriously about these things for our entire birthday month so we can come up with something brilliant. We've achieved many goals with this yearly tradition.

"I think it should be to completely let go of the past, and really, *truly* put your whole self out there for the world to see."

"I'm trying to find a version of myself I love enough to put out there."

"Well, maybe you have to loosen up a little more," she demands.

I laugh. "You're a real pain in my ass Stephanie Lawrence."

"I know. And I absolutely love it," she says. "Even though the two of us have grown up together side by side,

I'm a total extrovert, and you're much happier being an introvert. Let's meet in the middle and just unwind that duct tape you have holding you to the wall. We don't have to remove the stick up your ass too."

She says the words with such seriousness that it takes a second for them to sink in. I laugh hard, nearly chocking on my drink and sending it back out through my nose. Only Stephy can get away with saying these obnoxious things without getting into trouble.

"Maybe I need to start exercising more. I could join a Judo class."

"I think you need meditation more than fighting." She cocks her head. "Though, some ass kicking wouldn't be a bad idea. The tougher we feel, the more confident we are. It's also not a bad thing to be able to protect ourselves."

"I wonder what I'd do in a scary situation; would I be tough or curl up in a fetal position?"

"I think you'd shock yourself. When the going gets tough you've always been willing to run the extra mile."

"Not always. I curled up pretty hard after Bentley died."

"That's okay. We all have to allow ourselves to grieve." Before I can say anything, she keeps talking. "Your heart was broken, but it's had time to heal. Don't let life keep you in the dark. Embrace it. Embrace Sterling. I don't know if he's the one or not, but I do know he's the one *right now*. It can lead to more."

A bit of panic invades me. It's stupid. I've been with Sterling for months and I shouldn't be afraid to move forward. I don't think that's what's worrying me. I'm trying to make it permanent, but I know it won't be.

I think the thing that worries me the most is that I don't understand why. He's handsome, talented, funny, sexy, and he loves me. Sometimes I'll catch him looking at me and it absolutely takes my breath away. There's such devotion in his eyes.

"Okay, I'm going to listen to you as I always do. I'm going to try to let my anxiety go, and I'm going to try to make this my home for real and not look at it like a temporary situation."

"Just remember that someday we're going to be old and wrinkly, and our boobs are going to reach our belly buttons. We gotta lock in men long before that happens."

"I'm not worried about the wrinkles, or saggy boobs," I say with a giggle. "I don't want that nose and ear hair poking out in all of the wrong places, though."

Stephy spits out her drink as she bursts into laughter. "This is why I love you so much. Don't worry about the hair *or* the wrinkles. We'll zap them off."

"If anyone overhears us, they're going to think we're the most vain, obnoxious women in the world."

"Oh, trust me, we aren't even close," she assures me. "Hollywood actresses take the trophy home in pure vanity." I nod my agreement.

"Where did Sterling disappear to? I know he's giving us time to talk, but he's been gone a very long time," she says as she looks around.

"His brother's here. I think they're playing a game of pool."

Her eyes light up. "I have the perfect idea."

"I don't like that look in your eyes. Whenever you get it something bad happens . . . and usually to me."

She laughs again. "Of course something bad happens. It has to be bad to be interesting. Who thinks being good all of the time is any fun at all?"

"I think being good is great."

"That's because you're boring," she says with a wave.

"I'd rather be boring and safe, than fun and squished on the side of a mountain."

"I'd rather live, and I think you would too. Now, stop distracting me. I have a plan."

"Dare I ask what the plan is?" I reluctantly question her. I pick up my shot glass and down it. I have a feeling I'm going to need the liquid courage for whatever she has in mind.

"Go find your man but act as if you're just meeting him. Playing games has spiced up a lot of marriages. Go and hit on him as if he's a stranger. When he tries to talk to you as his wife, brush him off and tell him how sexy he is."

"I can't do that. I'm not good at games, and I certainly can't act. Besides, all I'd be thinking about is what people are thinking of me."

"Who cares about these people? You most likely will never see them again. That's the great thing about a city, you can go a little wild without anyone knowing who you are or even remembering your face the next morning," she tells me.

"Yeah, we can't do that at all in Prairie Town. News reaches home before we do."

"That's for sure. We never get away with anything at home, so we have to do it while we're here."

"Fine," I say, then get a wicked smile of my own. "But only if you find some stranger to go flirt with first." I think she might balk at this. Of course, I'm wrong.

"It's a deal. I've been eyeing several possibilities in this place. There's some sexy men at some bachelor parties at the bar."

"You are terrible. One of these days you're going to flirt with the wrong man."

"If a man is strong enough to tame me, he's one I want to know," she assures me.

"I don't think there's a man alive who can fit that description."

"Sadly, you might be right." We both stand.

I watch in awe as Stephy sashays right up to a group of men talking at the bar. She leans into one of them as if she's trying to reach the counter. She must say something extra flirty because one man's eyes widen as if he's won the golden ticket, then he parts the way for her to move forward. I'm too busy watching her to go seek Sterling out.

Within thirty seconds the bartender is there, and the man Stephy's flirting with is buying her a drink and has his arm wrapped around her. Man, is he going to be disappointed when he gets nothing more than flirting out of her. She can say all of the things she wants, but I have no doubt she won't go home with a single man tonight — she hasn't done it before.

I take in a breath and make my way across the crowded bar. This game seems insane, but I do feel a stirring of excitement as I seek Sterling out. Have I become a slut? Do I only get excited at the prospect of excitement and adventure? I hope not. I don't want to be that woman even though that's exactly who I am right now.

I break through the crowd, and there he is. He's sitting on a stool at the bar, his brother on one side of him, another man to his left. They are all laughing about something. He truly is a sexy man. His thick, dark hair is messed up as usual and tonight he's wearing a tight blue T-shirt that hides nothing of his wide shoulders and taut chest. It hugs him to his hips which are encased in dark jeans that make his ass and thighs deliciously hot. My stomach clenches as my mouth goes dry.

I take a step and realize I'm slightly wobbly on my feet. Maybe the last couple of shots weren't such a good idea. Then again, I'm feeling braver than normal. I'm just not sure I can pull off this game Stephy's insisting I play. Of course, she's quite occupied at the moment so if I can't pull it off, she'll never know.

I put one foot in front of the other as I move across the room toward Sterling. What am I going to say? How will I play this game? Ugh, Stephy is so much better at this stuff than I am. I should've watched her more closely over the years. I didn't think I needed to. I thought I had the love of my life and I'd never have to play games again. I was wrong. I was very, *very* wrong.

I move up behind Sterling. He hasn't figured out I'm here yet. I'm unsure what to do, what to say. Maybe I need to watch more romcoms so I can get this crap right. I totally fit the clueless, sweet, country girl that's in all of my favorites. Maybe that's because I can so clearly see myself in each and every role.

I clear my throat. I feel and see Sterling tense as I put a hand on his shoulder. He whips around as if he's about to slug someone. I'm shocked to realize I like this side of him. I like the tough guy act. Who would've known? Not me, that's for sure.

"Hey baby," he begins as he reaches for me. I lean forward and put a finger over his lips. His brother is having another conversation and not paying the least bit of attention to us.

"Shh, I . . . um . . ." I get irritated with myself. I can do this. It's just a game of pretend. It will be fun, I assure myself. "You look like someone I might've met before," I say with a flirty smile. His brows knit together in confusion.

"Char," he says. "What's going on?"

I have to think fast.

"Who's Char? I'm . . . um . . . I'm Wonder Woman," I say when I can't come up with anything better. I might as well scrap this whole game right now. I truly suck at it.

The confusion fades from Sterling's face as a grin widens across his lips.

"Wonder Woman, huh? I like it," he tells me. "So, what is Wonder Woman up to tonight? You look damn hot in your uniform." I'm wearing a short dress and low-slung heels. I'm comfortable and feel pretty good. I guess he likes it too.

I feel a flush heat my body. I'm off to a rocky start, but I like this. It's kind of fun. And it feels so much safer since it's not an actual stranger.

"I'm thirsty. Do you know a stranger who can buy a girl a drink?" I feel my cheeks flush. I've never used pick-up lines in my life and I'm sure I'm failing.

Sterling's smile grows bigger. He turns. "Go away," he says. His brother looks at him with a confused look, then sees me. His brother then laughs.

"As you wish. We're gonna play pool anyway," he says. He gets up and leaves.

"Your chariot, my darling," Sterling says as he pats his brother's stool.

I move to it and sit after nearly sliding over the slick plastic and landing on the bar floor. I'm just grace in motion at the moment. If I didn't already have this man, I'm not sure he'd still be talking to me. I'll never know.

"Ugh, I'm sucking at this," I say as he calls the bartender over and orders a couple of drinks. He then gives me his full attention as he leans in close.

"I'm hoping you'll be sucking at something tonight," he whispers in my ears. I flush all over my body as I look around. He's grinning even bigger now. I'm committed so I jump back into my role.

"That's awfully presumptuous of you. I'm not a girl to kiss and . . . more on the first date."

"Then we'd better make this ten dates in one night," he suggests. "Because you are the hottest thing I've ever seen in this bar, and I want to taste you from head to toe."

That heat in my body is now at volcanic levels. I'm burning, tingling, and ready to end the game and drag him to the nearest bathroom. I have to wonder who in the hell I am once again.

Our drinks arrive and Sterling gives me his full attention. "So, Wonder Woman, what brings you to this part of town?"

"I'm looking for a hot sexy guy." I'm growing more at ease. Okay, I can do it.

"I might know of one or two."

"Oh, you aren't available? Gay?" I say with a disappointed sigh. His eyes narrow.

"Really? I might need to prove my manhood if you keep that up."

I smile, meaning it this time. "Promises, promises." I'm growing hotter by the second.

Sterling reaches out and runs his finger down my arm. His hazel eyes are dark and heated, and the trail he's running down my skin is on fire. I reach out to him and touch his solid chest, appreciating his masculinity. Before I think about it I trail my hand down his abs then briefly graze the front of his pants where I'm delighted to find he's hard. I instantly grow wet.

"Let's move," he says in a low growl that goes straight to my stomach.

I don't get a chance to say a word as he leaps from the stool and pulls me down. I almost lose my drink but manage to keep it clutched in my free hand. He drags me through the crowd and finds an empty table in the back of the bar. He scoots behind it and slides me in close to him.

"It seems my little vixen wants to play games," he whispers in my ear.

"Aren't games fun?" I'm not sure where this is coming from, but I like it a lot.

"There are all kinds of fun games," he tells me as he leans down and runs his tongue against my pounding pulse. That makes it leap so hard I nearly jump in my seat.

I'm hot, I'm very, very hot. There's noise all around us, but we aren't paying attention to anyone, and people certainly aren't paying attention to us.

Sterling reaches down and slides his hand up my dress. My thighs shake. I try clenching them together, but he easily parts them the slightest bit. I'm panting as he holds me close, protecting my lower half from view as he slides up higher. I gasp as he slips a finger beneath the edge of my panties.

"Mmm, nice and hot . . . and wet," he murmurs in my ear before he licks my earlobe while sliding a finger inside of me. I nearly come from the contact.

"Sterling . . ."

"Shh, I'm Superman," he tells me before inserting another finger and slowly pumping in and out of me. I'm a little mortified as I've never done anything like this before in public, but I'm so damn turned on I can't find the will to stop what's happening.

"Yes, Superman," I gasp as his fingers pump faster and his thumb finds my sweet spot. I'm panting as I bury my head against his neck. I should stop this. I won't. It feels too good. He twirls his thumb as he pumps in and out of my heat, and then I bite down on his shoulder as I let out a guttural moan and my body explodes. I feel myself clench his fingers. The orgasm goes on and on and on and on until I finally turn to jelly in his arms.

It's several long moments before I look up at him. His eyes are on fire, and his body is rock hard. I want to go home, and I want to do it now. I want more. I *always* want more with this man.

"Has it been ten dates yet?"

It takes a minute for my muddled brain to comprehend what he's asking.

"Oh, it's been far more than ten." I smile. "I now want something bigger inside of me than your fingers."

He doesn't hesitate. He pulls down my dress and untucks his shirt to hide his huge arousal. He pulls me from my seat and begins walking through the bar.

"Wait, Stephy's here."

He groans. "Where?"

"The other side of the bar." He changes direction and practically drags me through the bar. We move right up to Stephy where she's laughing with a group of men.

"We're leaving," I say, still a bit breathless.

She laughs. "It seems you've found someone," she tells me with a wink.

"Yep," Sterling says as he holds out a hand. "Superman at your service." Stephy laughs hard at this. I'm thinking I'm dang glad it's not the hand he's just had inside my body. I think I might fall through the floor in embarrassment.

"It's a pleasure," she tells him. "You two take off. I won't be long." She winks. "Just long enough not to have my innocence shattered by you two breaking walls apart."

"Good idea," Sterling says.

We turn and practically run from the bar. We make it out to his truck in the back of the dark parking lot and we don't move for the next thirty minutes as he takes me in the backseat. I might never get enough of this man.

I want to feel this excitement, this heat, and this hunger every single day of my life. Maybe I can stay in New Orleans. Maybe I do truly just need to let go . . .

Chapter Twelve

I despised school dances when I was a student. I hated the fretting that went into them, the fear of not being asked to dance, the fear of doing something wrong. It's like a talent show where you're being judged the entire time you're there. Is my dress good enough? Have I done my hair right? What if no one talks to me? It's awful.

But then, I had that dance where Bentley pulled me into his arms and demanded I be his forever. That was one of my final school dances, and it was the best one of my life. I can't help but think of that day as I walk into the decorated gym of this school I've been teaching at for nearly eight months.

Has that much time passed already? Have I become an adult — a real-life adult, collecting a real paycheck, working Monday through Friday, grading my students, and spending time with my husband at night and on the weekends? Have I become completely domesticated?

That appears to be the case.

This is the final dance of the year for my students and both Sterling and I have been roped into chaperoning. I do have to smile at the theme of the dance — superheroes. The teachers aren't required to dress up, but of course we decide to. We haven't seen each other's costumes yet. We wanted it to be a surprise. I'm going to be highly disappointed if he doesn't do what I'm sure he's going to do. Why wouldn't either of us?

He drove to the school and I'm late and taking an uber. I want to walk in the doors and see his reaction. I want to feel more of the excitement I've been feeling these past few months as we flirt, as we play, as we grow more comfortable together.

The two of us might have started as strangers who did a crazy thing together, but we're close now. We respect one another and I think we love each another. No, it's not the same as how I feel about Bentley, but maybe I'm coming to realize that how I felt about my first husband is a once in a lifetime feeling. Maybe I can settle for less than what I had with him with someone new. Maybe that's perfectly okay.

I twinge at that thought. I don't want to think about it right now. As I step through the gym doors, I can't help but make comparisons though. Chaperoning this dance isn't a good idea. It reminds me too much of my deceased husband instead of thinking of the man I lie beside each night. It's not fair to Sterling. It's not fair to Bentley either. It's certainly not fair to me.

The PTA did a great job of decorating. I love it as I walk inside. Many students are already here, but hardly anyone is dancing. That's not unusual. Middle school kids are shy. They usually need some prompting to get going. That's okay, that's why most of the teachers decided to dress up, to encourage them to be themselves. About half of the students are in costume, while the other half are trying to pretend they're too cool for such silly games.

Finally, I spot Sterling by the food counter. My grin grows. There's my Superman. And hot damn if he doesn't look better than my favorite Superman of all time, the Christopher Reeve version. This man is damn fine . . . and I get to be the one to take him home tonight. My stomach clenches.

"Good evening, Mr. Worth," I say as I sidle up to him. He turns and his jaw drops.

"Damn, I'm a lucky man," he says with a long sigh as he looks at me from head to toe. I wasn't sure about this costume, but I'm dang glad I've worn it.

"I think Wonder Woman is my absolute favorite superhero of all time now."

This costume feels a little too revealing especially at a middle school dance, but it does cover all of the basics. I'm wearing tights, the bathing suit that hides all of my assets, and of course, all of the accessories. My favorite is the head band. I feel good.

"I guess we can have a battle and see who's tougher. I think Wonder Woman can take out Superman any day of the week."

"You won't get a single argument from me. I'm about to drop to my knees at just the sight of you. If you use your magical powers you'll surely win."

"Oh, you two are absolutely adorable," Mrs. Sine says with a sigh. "It makes me want to go and remind my husband we were both young and brave at one time. I might have to remind him tonight." She giggles like she's twenty-one instead of sixty-five. I love it.

"I'm sorry I'm late. I couldn't get my hair to cooperate."

"You're worth waiting for," he assures me. I know he means it.

"There's nobody dancing."

"Yeah, I think we're going to need to get them started."

"You want me to dance in front of all of these kids?" I gasp.

"It's okay, you can do it." He takes my hand and starts pulling me into the middle of the gym. I feel my cheeks heat. I shouldn't care what anyone thinks about me, but I'm suddenly embarrassed.

"I don't know if I can do this. I never have enjoyed dances."

"That's because everyone thinks everyone else is judging them when in reality everyone is scared and not worried about you, but themselves. If there happens to be someone being judgy, it's because they're an insecure person who is judging themselves more than anyone else.

Once we realize we're all hopelessly scared, we will start to dance like nobody's watching."

"I like that."

"Well, well, well, kids, it appears that Superman has gotten Wonder Woman onto the dance floor. Let's get this party started with a song," the DJ says. The Cha Cha Slide starts up and I throw back my head and laugh.

"I actually know the moves to this song." I'm feeling less nervous.

"Me too. I think it's against the rules to teach at a middle school and not know the moves to the cheesiest songs of all."

"I'm going to have to agree."

We start to dance, and I'm laughing. I'm having more fun than I thought possible. A few shy kids move onto the dance floor as they giggle with delight and start dancing with us. Sterling throws in a few twists and turns and gets cheered by the students.

"Come one, come all, don't let these old teachers show you up. Show them how this dance is done," the DJ commands. A slew of kids come out onto the dance floor and join us. Laughter is echoing inside the gym and everyone is having fun. I guess all it had taken was Sterling and me shaking our booties.

The song switches to The Harlem Shake, and the kids scream as they begin wiggling their bodies. When Sterling's arms drop to his sides and he shakes like a worm, I lose it, laughing so hard I find myself having a difficult time catching my breath. I'm sweaty by the end of the song.

We finally manage to get ourselves off of the dance floor and I head straight for the concession stand and beg for water, which is promptly handed over. The kids are still out there dancing, and everyone has seemed to loosen up.

"I think we've accomplished our goal. We shouldn't have to dance again." He sticks out his lip in a pout.

"Maybe I like a good dance."

"Well, if Cotton Eyed Joe comes on I might have to head out there once more. I do know all of the moves to that song too."

I think both of us are laughing more tonight than we have before. There's something about attending a middle school dance that makes us feel like kids again. Maybe we all need to find our inner child every once in a while.

The first slow song comes on and the floor empties fast. I laugh. I remember this quite clearly. A few brave students will eventually go out there, but as a girl, slow songs are painful. It sucks standing on the sidelines hoping to be asked to dance, praying not to be the only girl standing there all alone.

"Mrs. Worth?" I turn to find Sterling holding out his hand.

"Oh no." I take a step back.

"Oh, yes, I want to dance with my wife." He drags me out to the floor. I can't make a scene, so I have no choice but to follow him. I feel my cheeks heating knowing that all eyes are on us as *I've had the time of my life* plays over the loudspeakers.

"Everyone is looking at us," I whisper.

"That's because you're absolutely stunning."

"We're supposed to be supervising, making sure no one is spiking the punch, or sneaking off into the bathrooms."

"Maybe you and I will be the ones to sneak off into a nice quiet, dark room."

My body instantly responds to his words. I want to do just that. I want it very much. I want it enough that I'm forgetting all about the eyes that are all on us.

"How many chaperones are here?"

His eyes widen. "Are you planning on dragging me away, my beautiful wife?" He has hope and hunger in his expression.

"Oh, yes, Superman, I'm feeling very naughty, and I need some punishment for my bad thoughts."

Kids are finally trickling onto the dance floor. Sterling pulls me tightly against him for just a moment, letting me feel what my words are doing to him, then he pushes me back.

"I have to get myself under control before we leave this dance floor. This costume isn't very forgiving for a hard on," he whispers.

I laugh, realizing his predicament. "You can always turn your cape around," I say in between giggles. He glares at me. "Well, that's doing the trick," he says with a laugh. "Down boy." I laugh harder.

We keep dancing and then it comes to my favorite part of the song. He suddenly pushes me away. "Let's show these kids how truly young we are."

"No!" I'm emphatic. "No way. No how. Not going to happen. Do you hear me? No! No! No!"

He's not listening though, and it doesn't take long for the students to figure out what he's up to. They form a line on either side of us as he backs up and holds out his arms. The kids are cheering me. I have to do it. I'm left with no choice. I'm going to murder him . . . that is if he doesn't drop me on my head and kill me himself.

I start running toward him and the kids are screaming their encouragement. Sadly, I've seen this movie about twenty times so even though I've never done this move before I know exactly *what* to do. I step in front of him bend my knees then leap with his hands on my sides. He flings me up over his head as if he really is Superman and it takes him no effort at all. The kids are cheering. Even the other chaperones are clapping.

He lets me slide down the front of him and I meet his eyes, his sparkling, laughing eyes. He's having the time of his life, that's for dang sure. I have to admit it's pretty dang fun to live out a fantasy I've had for the past ten years.

"You say I'm trouble. I think you're the one who's trouble," I insist. Nothing he does that pushes me out of my comfort zone, though, has turned out bad. It's actually been pretty dang fantastic.

"Then I guess it's time for *me* to be punished," he tells me, his eyes so bright and excited it's like a beacon on a foggy sea. I will follow him anywhere if he keeps looking at me like this.

The kids are flooding the dance floor, and nobody is paying the least attention to us. I'm grateful for the short attention span of teenagers. Sterling and I manage to slip through the doors and head down the silent hallways of the school. He already has a key in his hand to enter his classroom. We slip inside and he instantly pins me to the door.

His mouth descends on mine and I'm lost in his touch. His hands caress my body while he wakes up all of my senses in the way only he can.

I'm suddenly lifted while his lips are still attached to mine. We're moving through the room until he sits me on his desk. He finally lets go of my mouth and stares at me, hunger burning in his expression.

"I've never wanted to do this in my classroom," he tells me as he begins partially stripping. "But if I don't have you now, I'll never make it through this dance."

"I had a crush on my math teacher in school. I always thought it might be a little sexy to have classroom sex." His eyes flare even more.

"I'll make you forget all about your old teacher," he assures me.

And he does! Mr. Mast is the furthest thing from my mind as he takes me to heaven again and again.

Sterling spends the next thirty minutes making me come as he caresses me with his hands and mouth. He tortures us both before he finally pulls aside my costume and plunges deep inside of me. My orgasm builds with nothing more than the feel of him connecting us. He begins to move and it's only a few strokes before I explode in his arms.

Everything that was on his desk is now scattered on the floor. Neither of us care. We lie there — partially costumed, partially nude — both utterly spent. I curl up against him as he caresses me. The door is locked so there's no fear of being interrupted, but we really should get back to the dance. I just can't seem to make my relaxed body do anything.

"Let's have a baby," he says.

His words take the breath right out of me . . . and not in a good way. My euphoria from just a second earlier has evaporated.

"A baby?" I pray I'm hearing him wrong.

He suddenly sits up so he's looming over me. "Yes, we're making this work, and I'm more than ready to be a father. I love you. I know we didn't start out in a conventional way, but you set my body on fire, you make me lose my breath, and you make my heart skip a beat. Let's be a *real* family."

There's so much love and laughter in his eyes as if he's just discovered the greatest gift in the world. I'm going to break his heart. Tears sting my eyes. I pull him close and kiss him, then tuck his head against my chest.

I know this is goodbye. I also know I don't want it to be. But that's only because I'm not ready to leave him . . . it's not because I want to stay forever.

I can't do this again. I can't hurt another man. I can't commit to someone when I know there will be no chance of a forever. I don't like causing pain just as I don't like feeling it. If I could take away the pain I'm going to put Sterling through, I gladly would. But no one can take the pain of a broken heart away from another.

I finally pull away from him and sit up. I straighten my costume. I'm not looking at him. I'm trying to find my words.

"You're a great man, Sterling." I turn and find him grinning. His costume is put back into place as best as it can be. "Let's go home."

He's smiling as he takes my hand and we leave the school. We don't bother to go back into the gym. There are plenty of chaperones. They don't need us. Me not saying anything about the baby makes him think I'm on board. That hurts me even more. I feel like every villain in every movie ever made. I'm worse because this isn't make-believe. A real heart will break tonight.

We get home and make love again, this time slow and sweet. I don't want to let him go. I want to remember this. I want to cherish these last few seconds together. Sterling falls asleep beside me, his head full of dreams and plans. Those will be shattered in the morning.

I climb from his bed and pack my one lone bag, then I write him a note:

I'm so sorry, Sterling. I'm sorry our time has come to an end. I love you, I really do, but I'm not the right woman for you. I can't give you those babies. I can't even give you forever. I've wronged you by staying so long. I should've explained to you how broken I really am. I should've ended it the first day we realized we were teaching together. But I didn't know what would happen. I don't regret a single moment of us being together. I loved it all. I hope you won't hate me. I hope you find the woman of your dreams and get the family you so desperately deserve. I do love you . . . it's just not enough.

With Love, Charlie

I leave the note, and I leave a feather. I don't know why. This is the second time I've done it. Maybe it's because even though these men don't realize I'm searching for my wings, I want them to somehow know I was never free to give myself to them. I want them to know they've helped unclip the wings from my back. I want them to know it's me, it's not them. Maybe someday it will all make sense . . . to them . . . and to me. I can hope.

I hang my head and walk out of Sterling's life. I don't look back. This time I have no regrets. How sad for him . . . and for me.

I send one quick message. *I'm coming home now.*

I know, is the only reply.

She knows. Stephy always knows. She knew months ago. I guess I did too. I just didn't realize it then. Only one tear slips as I call a cab and take a ride to the airport. I know Stephy will have a jet there soon. I'll wait. Maybe I'll wait forever . . .

Chapter Thirteen

There's dead silence in the courtroom as I finish my story. I find myself fighting tears. How am I feeling like this is happening right now when it's been about seven years ago? I don't know. For the first time I look out into the audience. I see Sterling sitting there. Our eyes meet. He gives me a half smile. I wonder what he's thinking. I don't have long to wait.

"We'd like to call Sterling Worth to the stand," Mr. Hart says, his voice almost gleeful. He's sure this time someone is going to trash me. He could be right. I hurt Sterling, probably more than I hurt any of them. I try not to have regrets, but I do hate that I've hurt this man.

Sterling is sworn in and I look up at him. He truly is a beautiful man with a great soul. Why couldn't I love him forever? Was I truly so broken at the age of eighteen that I'm unable to ever be fixed again? I sure hope not.

"Mr. Worth, do you feel deceived by Ms. Diamond?" Mr. Hart asks.

Sterling gives an indulgent smile. "No." He doesn't add more.

"What do you think of her today?" Mr. Hart asks, obviously disappointed in his first answer.

He pauses a moment as if he's really thinking about his answer.

"I think she's a beautiful soul who's been lost for a very long time. I think she's taken a journey through life many will judge and others will envy. I was simply a small chapter in that life. My time came and went. We both learned and grew from one another."

"You have zero resentment for her deceptions?" Mr. Hart pushes. Obviously this isn't going the way he wants it to go.

"I did," he admits. "I was sad and confused when she left. It took me some time to realize we were meant to be together for a little while, but that it was never meant to last. It was like holding on to an umbrella during a hurricane. You will eventually lose your grip."

"Why?" Mr. Hart asks.

"Why what?" Sterling questions.

"Why does it have to be difficult?"

Sterling laughs. "Have you ever dated?"

"Of course. However, I'm not the one on the stand."

"I don't think you'd do too well up here," Sterling says with another laugh. "Dating is like being a frog in a pot. You think it's all warm and cozy, and you don't realize you're slowly getting boiled. It might seem great in the beginning, but then suddenly you're boiled alive and it's too late to jump out. The only hope is the burner turns off, the pot gets tipped over, or a scoop lifts you to freedom. Dating should come with combat pay."

This makes the entire courtroom erupt in laughter. Anyone who's dated knows he's telling the truth. It can be great, but most of the time it's a nightmare. It's the man saying all the right words, and then bam, he's suddenly talking about his time in prison cooking in the kitchen, thinking it was a cool experience. It's also a fact that all of us women are crazy. We hide our crazy as best as we can, but these dang hormones make us have more mood swings than spiders have webs. Nobody knows anyone at first. When you learn of that person you gotta just hope he doesn't turn out to be a serial killer.

"I see here you're remarried," Mr. Hart says.

Sterling smiles. I feel . . . relief. I'm not sad he's moved on, I'm grateful he's found happiness. I'm very happy someone saw the superhero hiding within him. It's got to be a special woman as he's an incredible man.

"Yes, I've been married for four years now and I have a beautiful six-month-old daughter who looks like her mother," he says, pride shining in his eyes.

"But you're married to Ms. Diamond," Mr. Hart says, as if he's now going to prosecute Sterling. I'm not at all worried.

"No, I'm not," he says.

"We have a marriage certificate here," Mr. Hart says as he moves to his table and grabs a paper, holding it up as if he's got the Holy Grail.

"I don't know how, because if you look at the county records, there's no such thing filed in the courthouse. What you have a piece of paper that doesn't mean a thing. Trust me, I checked before I married my current wife."

Mr. Hart and the courtroom are dead silent at these words. Mr. Hart's case is falling apart with each new revelation. Cash turns and looks at me. I smile at him. He reaches over and squeezes my hand. I then see him turn toward Stephy for just a brief moment. He's beginning to figure out who she is. I hope he's strong enough to love her as she is and to not want to change her. Some men can't handle a woman like Stephy, a woman that confident and intelligent. I think Cash can.

"We're going to have to check on this, Your Honor," Mr. Hart says. He's definitely faster at recovering from shock than the old DA was.

"Take your time. It doesn't appear we're going to be getting out of here anytime soon," Judge Croesus says with an indulgent smile. This makes the audience laugh again. This hearing is turning into an outright comedy show.

"Your Honor, in light of the fact that all of the DA's so-called evidence is turning out to be false, I call to dismiss this case and release my client," Cash says as he stands.

"Your Honor, some of the key evidence might be disappearing, but we have far more. There's something in this case Ms. Diamond has messed up on. I'm sure of it. We demand to continue. She can't have been so thorough at cleaning up all of her illegal actions that we aren't going to be able to prove her guilt," Mr. Hart says.

Judge Croesus looks down at his notes before he glances up and meets both the eyes of Mr. Hart and then Cash.

"We'll continue," he says. There's a sigh in the audience. I don't think anyone wants this to end. More people want to hear the story than don't. I don't think I'm ready to stop telling my story. Do I need the world to hear it? Maybe. I'm not sure yet. I could just sit down with Stephy, with my parents, and with all of my husbands. But somehow it feels safer to speak from the witness stand as if I remove myself from the situation.

"I reserve the right to call this witness back," Mr. Hart finally says. I can see a sleepless weekend for him. The poor man keeps taking two steps back for every single one forward.

"Do you have any questions, Mr. Abernathy?" the judge asks. Cash stands.

"Did you love Ms. Sapphire?" he asks, using the name I was with Sterling. I look up and meet Sterling's eyes again. He nods.

"I loved her very much. There will always be a piece of me that will. I'm very in love with my wife, and I thank Ms. Sapphire for opening me up to love so when McKenzie came along I was ready for her," he answers.

"Thank you. I have no further questions," Cash says.

"Courts dismissed for the day," Judge Croesus says. He bangs his gavel and instant chatter starts in the courtroom.

I watch Sterling walk past my table. I'm not sure if he's going to talk to me or not. It hurts to think that this might be the last words I ever hear from him.

Cash gathers his papers and I stand. I turn and see Sterling is still in the courtroom. Several of the reporters are too. I decide not to hide. I move up to him and stop about three feet away. I can hear the quiet click of shutters as reporters zero in on this exchange. Who knows what they will say about it in tonight's headlines.

"Hello, Charlie," Sterling says. He has his arm wrapped around a petite brunette. I can't really read either of their expressions.

"Hello, Superman," I say. I know it's probably wrong, but I can't help myself. He looks far more like Clark Kent at the moment, but he'll always be Superman to me.

"I'd like you to meet my wife, McKenzie."

"Hello," I say. I don't hold out my hand. I have a feeling she has no desire to shake it. She looks as if she's not going to let go of her husband, as if she's afraid I might try to take him back. Is that how the world is looking at me now? It breaks my heart to think anyone might see me as that person, the person to ruin another's marriage. I just seem to destroy my own, not go after men who are already taken.

"I hated you for a while," McKenzie says. Sterling squeezes her even as he winces. I deserve this. She has a right to say whatever she wants.

"I understand. I'm sure it's not easy to sit here and hear about the past," I say with true empathy.

"When I met Sterling a couple years after you left, he was still sad. He didn't understand why you'd gone when everything was so good. He's had time to heal. Being here has been very good for him. He understands now."

She pauses for a long moment. I know she has more to say so I wait.

"I understand too. Even when we aren't here, I've watched the hearing. I'm sorry for the losses you've gone through. I'm sorry for the journey you've had to take." Again, she pauses. She then smiles at me. "I'm a little jealous if I'm going to be honest," she finally admits.

"Jealous?" This I haven't expected.

"Yes, you've lived a dozen lives in as many years. You've seen the world. You've found yourself. I might not agree with everything you've done, but it's not my right to judge you. That's between you and those you love and those who love you. I'm glad you've found yourself and beaten the pain. I hope the end of your journey is as great as the route you've taken."

The tears I've fought all afternoon slide down my cheeks. I can no longer hold them back. This stranger. This woman I most likely will never see again, has touched me, and understands me more than I really understand myself.

"Thank you," I choke out. "This means a lot to me. I hope the two of you have a beautiful life together."

"You changed me, Charlie, you helped me break free from myself. I don't regret a minute of our time together. I hope you do find that person who makes you fly. I'm starting to see your wings," Sterling says. He reaches in his pocket and pulls out a weathered feather. I'm in shock. He hands it to me. "You've left pieces of yourself behind everywhere you've been. Maybe it's time to put yourself back together again."

I want to hug him badly, but I stay where I'm at. They're leaving today. I won't see this man again. It saddens me . . . I know it's the way it's supposed to be.

"Thank you for what you've given me. I'm so glad I've gotten to see you again." I turn and look at McKenzie. "Take care of him better than I ever could."

She chuckles. "That's my plan. He's my rock, and I hope to always be as strong as he is."

I nod. They turn and walk away. Stephy and Cash walk up beside me. I'm looking at the floor.

"You sure know how to pick them," Stephy says. I look up and give her a watery smile.

"I sure do. I just don't understand why I don't want to hold onto them. Maybe I don't know how to properly tie a knot."

Cash laughs. "I don't think that's the problem, Charlie. I think the winds have simply been too strong to hold you down. Maybe we have to look for a better anchor."

"I did enjoy my time fishing in Florida." I smile. "But even that wasn't enough to hold me."

"It's not over," Stephy assures me as she wraps her arm around me.

I look up in time to see Sterling and McKenzie slip from the courtroom. I know the press is waiting outside, hoping we'll stop and talk.

"Do you want to go out the front or the side door?" Cash asks. I wonder if Sterling will say some words to the press. I realize I'm okay with it. I'm okay with all of the men talking. Just as I've gotten to tell my story, they deserve to do the same.

I stand there and let the last of my tears fall before I wipe my cheeks and firm my shoulders. I've sworn I won't hide anymore.

"The front," I finally say.

I move forward with Cash on one side of me, and Stephy on the other. I can do this. I can see this through. It's time to move to the next chapter of my life.

Chapter Fourteen

I'm back at Bentley's grave. I'll always come back. I always need to come back.

I take a sip of my wine and let the last tear I'm allowing on this day to fall. I wipe my cheeks and gaze at Bentley's tombstone. It's as beautiful as ever. Stephy never allows it to get dirty. She never allows the grounds to be less than perfect. This is an oasis in the desert surrounding it.

"Why did you love me so much? Do you still love me? Are you looking down from heaven and wondering who I am? I'm wondering. I wonder every single day. I keep telling myself I'm not going to be this woman, but then I do something over and over that is the opposite of what I say I'm going to do. I'm hurting people; I'm hurting myself. Is it because I miss you so much? I wish I knew. I wish you could talk to me and help me figure it out like you always used to."

"I think he does answer you," Stephy says as she kneels down next to me. "You just second guess yourself and want to be wrong. I think you want to find yourself evil. That's not how Bentley ever saw you, and it's not how I see you."

"If my parents knew who I've become, I don't know that they'd ever talk to me again. We have to stop this, Stephy. I can't keep this up."

My face is dry. I'm done crying.

"I think a parent loves their child no matter what journey they take in life. A parent might not always *like* their child, but they always *love* them. It's okay to be unique. You are living your life; that's okay too."

"I'm not going to a new location," I tell her. I'm emphatic.

"You're hurting right now." She pauses for a long moment. "How about we go to the next place together?"

I perk up. "You'll come with me somewhere?" It's practically a plea.

She laughs. "I need to get out of this town for a while. I've wanted you to grow, but I haven't realized that I need to grow too. I love myself. But I'm miserable right now. I can do my job from anywhere in the world, so why not go somewhere and be free?"

"Yes, yes, yes, let's go somewhere together. I don't want to find another man. I just want to be somewhere and find myself. There's nothing wrong with that."

She wraps her arms around me. "No, there's nothing wrong with that. But the next place we're going might change your mind. I've heard there's love in the air," she says with a giggle.

"I'm not sure I trust that look in your eyes. You're up to no good."

"I'm always up to no good. But that's what makes life fun."

"Where are we going? What will my job be? I have to admit I have fun doing different jobs."

"I know you do. When you talk to me about your work, you light up brighter than a Christmas tree. I love it. I think you'll really love this new one."

She stops. I let out a frustrated breath. "So, tell me."

She only pauses a moment longer. "We're heading to Italy where you have a job at a vineyard. Your new name starting in three months is Charlie Jade."

It takes a little while for her words to sink in, and then I find myself smiling. "Italy? Really? You aren't teasing?"

I'm going to be devastated if she's not serious. "I'm not teasing."

"But I don't have a passport. I don't know anything about international travel."

She laughs. "A passport? Really, Charlie? Do you not know me at all?" She pulls a passport from her bag and hands it to me. There it is, Charlie Jade, twenty-two-year-old woman with zero stamps on the pages.

"I get to be my real age now?" I laugh.

"Well, since we're both over twenty-one I figure we'll keep your age what you are. That way we don't have these super old men trying to home in on you."

"I don't think they care about age." Then I grow serious. "I'm telling you right now, I'm not looking for a man, not getting into a relationship, and under no circumstances am I getting married again! I want you to nod. I want you to acknowledge that you understand and you know how serious I am."

We stare each other down for several moments. She finally laughs.

"I acknowledge you *think* you're in control of your life. But, the beauty of being free is that we get to make choices and we get to change our minds. You never know what's going to happen."

We both stand and walk back to our horses that are grazing. They are beauties. We climb on them and begin riding farther out into the hills. I have a need to run until I leave all of my troubles behind me.

"I guarantee I know what's going to happen. I'm going to spend a wonderful year in a foreign country for the first time in my life. I'm going to be free and happy. I'm going to swim in the ocean, catch lots of fish, and fall in love with . . . pasta. Then I'll come back home refreshed and an entirely new woman."

"Good luck with that." She hits the back of her horse and darts off in front of me. I laugh. I know who I am . . . I think. I'm going to do what I say. Nothing is going to change my mind this time. It hurt too much leaving Sterling; I'm not going to do it to another man again.

I kick my horse and chase after my best friend. I love this place. This will *always* be home. The world might be calling me, but home will forever be that beacon that draws me back, no matter how far I manage to travel from it.

I'll find my happiness even if I have moments of utter despair. That's life. That's how it's supposed to be. In a few months, I'll be in Italy. I wonder what the next adventure will look like. I guess I'll find out.

Epilogue

Court was draining today. Mr. Hart hammered me, trying to get me to change my story, trying to find something that will land me in prison. He's failing. He'll continue to fail. I have Stephy on my side — no one can touch me. That doesn't mean it doesn't get to me, that doesn't mean I don't get wiped out. It means I hopefully won't go to prison.

There's a knock on the door. Stephy and Cash are gone. I'm not expecting anyone else, but maybe it's my mother. I could use her comfort right now. I don't deserve it. I've promised myself I won't have regrets. I've promised myself I won't feel guilty. But after going through the trial and talking about Sterling, how could I not? How could I have done that to such a good man?

Sterling is happy now. He's married. He has a daughter. But there was a time I hurt him. Can I consider myself a good person when I've hurt so many? Stephy tells me people get together and break up all of the time, and someone is bound to be hurt, but I feel I've done it more than most. What does that make me?

I open the door and am shocked to find *him* here. I can't even think his name without regrets. I can't say it. I haven't expected him.

Why? How? I don't know what to say. We gaze at each other for several moments. I finally open the door up so he can step inside. I move to the couch and sit. I don't know what this is, I don't know what he'll say.

"Charlie, I can't stay away. I can't stop watching the hearing," he tells me.

"I know. I've seen you. You must hate me," I say. I fight back tears. He doesn't say anything. I finally look up and meet his gaze. I'm shocked by his expression.

"No, Charlie, I understand you more each day." I wait. He doesn't add more.

"What do you mean?"

"I fell in love with you in a single heartbeat. I *still* love you. But you never let me in. Now, you're letting the world in. Now, I'm getting to know the real you."

I'm shocked. "How?" It's the only thing I can think to say. I don't think I even know the real me.

"You might not be able to see yourself as I see you, or as the world sees you, but that doesn't mean you aren't the woman I fell in love with."

I think about his words for several moments.

"I'm not the same woman you met."

"No, you aren't. You're stronger. You're better."

"I am stronger," I say. "But I'm also shattered. The good and bad come in equal measures."

He smiles. He has a smile that can light up a cavern. It's beautiful, comforting, and manly all in one. "We will be together," he says. There's such confidence in his words that I almost believe him.

I gasp. This isn't what I've expected him to say. He smiles at me. He then leans forward and presses his lips to mine, and I feel that spark, that heat, that tingling in my gut that no other man has made me feel. I've felt passion, and lust, and need, and love, but with this man, there was always something else.

I still walked away from him though. What does that mean? What does any of it mean?

"You'll see. Finish telling your story, Charlie. You need to tell your story. I think you're going to find your own answers as you do. You'll see that it will all be okay in the end."

He doesn't give me time to answer. He stands and walks back out of my room. I sit where I am for a very long time. When I finally get up again, I wonder if he really just came to me or if it was merely a dream. I'm not quite sure.

He's the one man I haven't forgotten . . . not for a moment, not from the first glance I had of him. But what does this mean. Will he back? Do I want him back? Does he really want me? Or is this a long game of retaliation? Does he want me back so he can walk away? I sit and sit, still not finding the answers.

I guess only time will tell . . .

Made in United States
Orlando, FL
02 November 2021